DESERT EAGLE

A SINATRA THRILLER

ALAN LEE

Desert Eagle

A Sinatra Thriller

by Alan Lee

First Edition
Printed in USA
9798360898351

Cover by Damonza

Formatting by Vellum

Sparkle Press

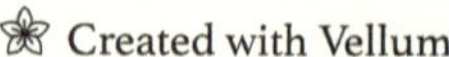 Created with Vellum

MERE STONES

We who cut mere stones must always be imagining cathedrals.
-Quarry Workers' Creed

Dear Reader,

Some of Manny's life takes place 'off screen,' inside another series, the Mackenzie August mysteries. Most readers of Sinatra also read Mackenzie, but in case you haven't, this book contains a prologue with a scene from the eleventh Mackenzie novel, *Dirty Deals*. The scene is short, and will help explain Manny's world as this novel begins.

Enjoy.

PROLOGUE

The unlikely pair of Deputy US Marshal Manny Martinez and NSA analyst Noelle Beck arrived in separate cars for dinner at the August household. Noelle had only just returned from three personal days, taken because her long-time suitor Rocky Rickard was in town to see her. With no time to catch up, she and Manny exchanged awkward pleas-antries at the front door, Noelle absorbing the expected good-natured ribbing about her boyfriend.

Mackenzie called for order and explained the dinner—a salad buffet. Start *here*, filling your plate as you go, and end *there*, at the salad dressing. Manny forced Noelle to go first and had strong opinions on her choices—get the romaine, not the iceberg, skip chicken in favor of cubed steak, avoid onion strips, go for the veggies, and generously apply vinai-grette dressing for the good fats. As always, Noelle was nervous under the attention of this group, especially Veronica Summers and Sheriff Stackhouse, women older than her and impossibly more sophisticated and beautiful.

All diners seated with a plate of their own bricolage,

Mackenzie's gorgeous two-year-old son (or was he three? No, couldn't be) held up his juice and said, "Cheers!" and the table returned the gesture. Mackenzie asked each person to share about his or her day and focus on the eudaemonic, whatever that meant.

Timothy August, the elementary principal and patriarch of the group, stated that his school was entirely free of students and teachers during this portion of the summer, and it was pure bliss.

Stackhouse, holding hands with Timothy, said that her sheriff's department was undergoing a state audit, and her staff hated her as they worked through lunch.

Veronica Summers' afternoon clients canceled and she returned home for an impromptu nap with Mackenzie.

Mackenzie said during the nap he tried something romantic but it failed.

Manny arrested Melanie Vasquez at a 7-Eleven buying fraudulent money orders. He'd been after her for weeks, Noelle knew, and he complained that he processed the paperwork himself because Beck was vacationing with a known criminal kingpin.

It was her turn. A cold dread in her stomach caused her hands to shake.

She set down the fork and wiped her mouth. Cleared her throat and wondered if the universe had ever been this quiet before.

Better to get it over with.

"Rocky Rickard proposed today," she said.

Manny sat straighter in his chair.

Stackhouse knocked her wine glass forward but caught it, sloshing a drop of cabernet.

"*Proposed?*" said Timothy August. He wiped his mouth too. "Congratulations. Was this expected?"

Noelle managed a smile. Part of it genuine.

"It was not. At all."

"How exciting," said Ronnie. "Where? When? How?"

"*Cheers!*" said Kix.

Manny took a long drink on a bottle of low carb IPA. When he lowered it, the bottle make a soft sucking sound. "Bought her a blood diamond with blood money, I bet."

Noelle didn't look at him. Her cheeks were pink, she knew. "It's not a blood diamond, you dork."

"When?" said Ronnie.

"Today, before he left for Washington."

"Aren't we forgetting the most important part?" demanded Stackhouse. "What did you say, babe?"

Noelle's left hand still held the glass of water. She wore no engagement ring.

"I bet she said yes and now she's the new *Viuda Negra*, queen of the drug cartels," said Manny.

"Rocky has divested himself of all his illegal enterprises. He's sold numerous companies and informed his former colleagues that he's a legitimate businessman now." Noelle's voice sounded pathetically defensive to her own ears and she hated it.

Manny made a snort.

"And he's not doing it solely for me," she continued. "He started the process before we met."

Stackhouse turned up her palm. "You said yes?"

"I... I didn't say anything. He told me not to."

"Details," said Ronnie. "I need details."

"I accompanied him to the airport." Noelle smiled, fully genuine now. "He owns a private jet. A Cessna."

"Killed the former owner," said Manny.

"He did not. Anyway. He asked to show me the interior

of the jet. A table was set inside with champagne and the ring," she said.

"Oh my." Ronnie leaned backward in her chair and took a deep breath. "That's sexy as hell."

Stackhouse patted the table impatiently. "He told you not to respond?"

"He said I could leave with him right then. But if I wasn't ready, I should think it over. So I am."

"I'm surprised the *pendejo* didn't have you shot," said Manny.

"Good for you, babe." Stackhouse picked up her wine goblet and raised it to her. "You hooked a big one, and you're taking your time."

"Thank you." Her smile dimmed. "It's a lot. The whole thing, it's... It's a lot. I'm not thinking clearly."

Manny shook his head and make a tsk'ing noise. "Your mom's gonna have a fit."

"She's going to have two fits," said Noelle. She wouldn't be telling her anytime soon.

"Cheers!"

"If you want to talk it over, I'll clear my schedule," said Ronnie.

Noelle felt a rush of pleasure. *The* Ronnie Summers. "Yes please, Ronnie.

"Do you love him?" said Stackhouse.

"I don't *know*. No? Maybe? Isn't love supposed to be something you do, not only an emotion? If I say yes, then I'll begin to love him?" Noelle shrugged and let the heaviness of it stoop her shoulders, and she pointed at Stackhouse and Timothy. "Why aren't you two married? When will you know it's time?"

The room jumped, like hit with a jolt of electricity.

Manny leaned away from Beck. "*Ay dios mio.*"

"Holy moly," said Mackenzie.

She'd said something wrong, she knew, *rats*, she tried so hard not to. Yet she always seemed to do this.

"Sorry, is that off limits?" Noelle looked around for help. "I feel like I walked into a minefield."

Stackhouse and Timothy grinned at each other, like they enjoyed the discomfort.

"This is wonderful." Ronnie finished her wine and set it down, smiling. "I've wanted to ask that question for two years at least."

"There's no great secret to it, babe," said Stackhouse. "We're both happy with the way things are."

"But would marriage make us happier?" Timothy asked her.

"Maybe, maybe not." Stackhouse canted her head side to side. "I feel oddly lucky and blessed to have this handsome man, and I'll take him as long as I can get him."

Across the table from Noelle, Mackenzie and Ronnie appeared to be sharing their own private, quiet joke, watching the elder couple.

"My looks are already fading," continued Stackhouse. "And his perfect young teachers are looking more gorgeous by the day, I assume. They adore him like I do, so until a day comes that he wants to trade me in, I'll count my blessings."

"Your looks are not fading," said Timothy August. "I'm the lucky one. You are the catch."

She nudged him with a shoulder. "Aren't we maudlin and disgusting."

"Yes," said Mackenzie. "Yes you are."

"I'm the best I've ever been when I'm with Timothy. He makes me a better person," Stackhouse told Noelle. "If he ever proposes, I'll say yes. But we're old, babe. Don't use us for an example."

"He makes you a better person." Ronnie tilted her head back and spoke at the ceiling, mostly to herself. "That's it, isn't it. Making him better. Making me better. Or at least, that's a lot of it. But how do you explain that to someone who is self-centered."

"That self-centered comment better not be about me, *señorita*." Manny took his plate to the sink, food half finished. He washed the dish, his movements too loud and forceful. "Cause I'm feeling so generous I might walk Beck down the aisle."

"I didn't ask you to," said Noelle. The ways of Manny Martinez were a mystery, but not the anger. You knew it when he was.

"No man gets you unless I give you away, Beck."

The possessiveness stung her. Irritated her.

"Of course Manny Martinez wants to be the focal point of someone else's wedding. Even mine," said Noelle.

"Better not tell Rocky's guests I'm coming. None of them will show up."

"Maybe you won't receive an invitation."

"Gonna be embarrassing I arrest him at the alter," said Manny.

"He's not a..." No, she wouldn't argue the point again. She knew a portion of Rocky's fortune came from illegitimate business practices, from organized crime, but there was nothing she could do about his past. And besides, he'd promised he was done with that life. She would not give Manny the satisfaction of yelling about it. "It's been a long day, and I need to leave. Thank you for dinner."

Noelle walked quickly to the front door, and it opened on silken hinges.

Manny muttered something under his breath and he stomped up the rear staircase. With a final glare, Noelle closed the door behind her, both gone and leaving behind tomes of obvious and unspoken words.

Stackhouse sighed. "Those two."

1
___

Manny Martinez was eating breakfast *al fresco* at Scrambled —late summer in downtown Roanoke demanded outdoor eggs. A covey of tables were served through a swinging door by an industrious waitress named Kiera, and Manny was on his second order of the southwest scramble.

Across from him sat Marcus Morgan. Tall and austere and handsome, Morgan wore mostly black with silver highlights—an earring, a necklace, a TAG Heuer watch, and the unnecessary Ray-Bans, in whose mirrored surface Manny could watch himself. Morgan had finished his vanilla pancakes and was drinking coffee.

"When is the wedding?" he said.

Manny waved a fork. "I don't know. Neither wants a big ceremony. Speaks well of them, you ask me. No need to celebrate yourself. One day they'll elope to some island, and that'll be it."

Another man sat at the table. Lonnie Cox. He watched without eating or speaking, and he looked sullen about it. He was a small-time thug, making a bad living by boosting cars in bad neighborhoods.

He didn't work for Marcus Morgan. Marcus Morgan trafficked only in cocaine.

"You don't love her," said Marcus.

"No. I don't love Beck."

"But."

"Mackenzie says I don't want anyone else to love her either." Manny leaned backward in his chair and stretched to work out the irritation between his shoulders.

"Sound to me like love. It ain't friendship."

Manny nodded to the street, where his black Camaro glistened with a recent waxing, so sleek and polished the car looked fluid. "Ay, see that? I don't *love* the car. But that don't mean I want a lot of people driving it. Don't mean I want to give it away."

"You love that car."

"I respect the car. American ingenuity," said Manny. "I love America. Despite her faults, I love her still."

Lonnie Cox looked nervously between the two men.

Kiera returned to fill their coffees. She smiled and asked if they needed anything else, and Manny said no, just the check.

"So you invited me to breakfast to discuss Noelle Beck's upcoming marriage." Marcus's voice was like a deep sound that came out of a long underground tunnel.

"No."

"All we talked about," said Marcus.

"You brought it up, *amigo*."

"Wish I hadn't."

"Let's talk then. About a guy named Doyle," said Manny. Lonnie Cox stiffened. "You know him."

"Yeah I know Doyle," said Marcus. "Know of him."

"Tell me what you know."

"Why would I do that?"

Manny made a shrug and poured some cream into his coffee. He had to keep doing it, because Kiera refilled his mug too often. "Because you and me, we're on the same side."

"You the marshal, and me the, ah, businessman," said Marcus.

"And Doyle, the new *pendejo* making me angry."

"How about this, Marshal," said Marcus. "How about you go first. Tell me what you know about Doyle."

"*Bien*. Doyle, he's Irish. Comes from Boston organized crime, relative of the O'Callahan family. The RICO Act busted up their racketeering gig, and half the family is in prison, but Doyle came south. This is District King territory, though. He's working his way into their good graces with gambling, working out of Roanoke because here you control east to Richmond, south to Charlotte, west to Lexington, and north to... *ay dios*, I don't know, Pittsburgh? Big damn area."

"Not just gambling. Doyle's funneling in crack," said Marcus.

"Crack. I hate crack."

"I know."

"Where's he getting it?"

"Any fool can make bad crack. This stuff, it's not from me or my crew. It's not homemade. You know how to tell quick? The good stuff sinks in water. Doyle's product is pure, not cut. Boston connection, maybe."

Manny indicated them both with his mug. "We keep crack out of our city."

"We do. Not at the moment, though."

"Where is he?"

"Not sure," said Marcus. "Somewhere close. What I hear. But he's already deep. Hidden. Got a team in place."

"You criminals don't have a group chat."

"No we don't have a group chat."

"You can't call him up," said Manny.

"Irish piece of shit is avoiding me. Smart man."

"Who's his District Kings connection?"

"Someone higher up than me," said Marcus.

Frustration was warm in Manny's chest, like a simmering furnace.

"You're small potatoes in the Kings?" he said.

"I look like small potatoes? Not a lot of folks higher up. But some."

"If you find Doyle, you'll kill him?"

Marcus grinned. He used his napkin to wipe up a spot of coffee on the table. "I'm a respected businessman, Marshal."

"Las pendejadas."

"Here's how it is." Marcus dropped the napkin and hoisted the heavy mug. "See. This coffee, it's Roanoke. And it's mine. Get that? Everyone knows. I'm holding it, and everyone knows it. Doyle, he's this cup of cream." Marcus picked up the little tumbler of half & half. "Doyle's doing his thing over there, separate from me, cause like I said, he's smart. But he's slowly adding himself." Marcus poured some cream. "Mixing himself in. Little by little. Once the coffee was black. Now it's less black. Soon it'll be even less black. Right now, it's okay. It's good. District Kings like it. Kings like the way it tastes right now. They don't wanna rock the boat. They like it better than when it was black."

"Kings are making more money this way," said Manny, "with gambling and candy."

"Think so. Think he's got a connection higher up than me and he's slipping them cash. So I tell the Kings I don't like this Irishman, I don't want crack in my city, you know what they say?"

"Nothing good," said Manny.

"Nothing good."

"So the Kings won't help you. Maybe they want the Irishman to win cause they'll make more."

Marcus set the coffee and the cream down. "They would make more. Cause I got scruples Doyle don't."

"And you won't kill him."

"Didn't say that. I said I'm a businessman," said Marcus.

"Find out some things for me, *sí*? Help me and I'll put him away. I lock his ass up in Guantanamo Bay, I have to."

"Not gone be easy, Marshal. And I can't find out anything quick. This ain't a problem we solve this week. Or this month."

"Listen," said Lonnie Cox, speaking for the first time in twenty minutes. He raised his hands from his lap. They were handcuffed and tethered to the chair. "Can I call a lawyer? Or let me go? I promise I won't do it again, sir."

Kiera brought the check and Manny paid. At the bottom of the bill was Kiera's phone number, if Manny wanted to see the new Mission Impossible movie sometime, or anything else. Manny unlocked Lonnie from the chair and they both stood.

"Do some research, *amigo*," he said.

Marcus nodded, his mirrored Ray-Bans catching sunlight. "Let's meet again in a month. See what happens."

"Put me on speed dial. You see him, press my button. I don't play politics," said Manny.

Marcus grinned. Perfect white teeth.

"Why I like you, Marshal. Good old-fashioned muscle, doing shit most won't. 'Sept you got a badge."

❧

Lonnie Cox rode silently in the Camaro across town. Like everyone who knew of Manny Martinez, he was scared of him. Martinez had a reputation of handling the underworld rough. Often arresting a man, keeping the man a couple hours, and then releasing him, the man worse for wear and wishing he'd been locked up instead. Multiple allegations of police brutality had slid off his back because Martinez had a way of proving the men he caught were guilty as sin and had resisted arrest, which was more or less true. Plus, somehow Martinez's reputation was impervious enough, the good he did monumental enough, that he was untouchable.

Lonnie Cox didn't speak, and he regretted doing it at breakfast. He'd been caught red-handed by a man who could do whatever he wanted. And, though impossible, Martinez seemed to be even more fearsome than the tall tales. There was a wild otherness to him, a sense that he was only pretending to be domesticated, a wolf in cops' clothing. The tattoos and the muscles and the hair and the clenching jaw, Cox hoped if he remained quiet he'd make it out of the man's Camaro alive. He was desperate, *frantic*, to call a lawyer.

Martinez buzzed his window down and swiped a card for access to the Poff Building, and the barricades lowered. The Camaro pulsed through and Manny parked.

Cox swallowed and stared ahead. Manny killed the engine and they simmered in silence a minute.

"I know your momma," said Manny.

Cox jumped. "What?"

"*Tu madre.* I know your momma. Good woman, named Alyssa. Works two jobs."

"Her name's Aniyah, sir," said Cox.

"Don't speak, Cox."

"Aight, my bad."

"I know Alyssa and we worked a thing out last year, cause she told me her story, and I check on her now and then and she's doing good, Cox."

"Yes sir. Yes sir she is."

"She's still working at the Carilion laundromat?"

"Yes sir, most nights," said Cox.

"And I find her son," said Manny, "I find her son *hijacking cars*."

Manny shouted the words and Cox flinched away from him. He hit his head on the Camaro's window and cursed.

"The hell you doing, *cabron*, boosting cars, your momma working so hard to make a good life," said Manny.

"I'm sorry about it."

"You understand sacrifice?"

"Sir?"

"You get the sacrifice your momma's making? Sacrificing her life for yours. Working hard for you," said Manny. "You understand it?"

"Yes sir, and I'm sorry."

"You owe money?"

Cox swallowed and nodded.

"How old are you? Twenty?" said Manny.

"Nineteen."

"Nineteen. Already boosting cars, nineteen, *maldita*," said Manny. "Who do you owe?"

"I owe some to Crazy Kay."

"Crazy Kay. Guy with half his bottom lip cut off."

"Yes sir, that's him," said Cox.

"Who does Crazy Kay work for?"

"No one, I don't guess."

"Everyone works for someone, Cox. Where's your dad?"

"What?" said Cox.

"*Dónde está tu papi?*"

Cox swallowed again.

"I don't know, sir."

"Mine's gone too, Cox."

"What?"

Manny's phone buzzed. He paid no attention but it buzzed again and Manny sighed and checked. Read the message, his face catching some of the screen's glow.

"Get out," said Manny.

Cox obeyed quickly, standing into the warm morning light. Manny came around the Camaro and undid the cuffs, metal rasping

"Lucky for you, Cox, I like your momma. And lucky for you I gotta go. Else I might beat you with a hose for running away, *tú entiendes*?"

"I didn't run away, sir. I wouldn't—"

"You understand, Cox?" said Manny.

"Oh yes sir, I understand, sir."

"Pay back what you owe to Crazy Kay, *amigo*."

Cox made a jerking, nodding motion.

"Okay?" said Manny.

"I'll try. I will."

"You better. Guy's missing some of his face. Seems like he's got anger issues, Cox," said Manny.

"Yes sir."

"You take two jobs. Understand? Take two jobs, like your mom, whatever her name is, and pay it back. You can't get a job, call me. And you tell Crazy Kay, Manny Martinez says you get an extension. You follow?"

"You want me to tell Crazy Kay... What?"

Manny shook his head, a muscle in his jaw working.

"Don't be a little bitch about this, Cox. You're a man now. Dumbass man, but still. Ay. Tell Crazy Kay that Manny

Martinez says you gotta pay it all back but you get an extension, and I'll be around soon. You follow all that?"

"Y-yes sir, I do," said Cox. "Tell him I got an extension from Manny Martinez and you'll come around soon."

"You know the reason you're not in jail?"

"My mom?"

"Cause of your mom's sacrifice. And you keep calling me sir. I like manners so much, *amigo*, it's what makes America great." Manny gave him a little shove and when Cox turned he smacked Cox on the ass hard enough to make his eyes water. "*Vamos..* Tell your momma hi from me, same with Crazy Kay. Go on, run."

Cox stumbled and turned to thank Manny for letting him go, but Martinez was already halfway to the doors leading into the tall, monolithic Poff Building, looking at his phone, and Cox wondered about the nature of the text message Manny received. And about the man himself.

2

———

The second floor of the Poff Building was a hard, ugly place, like most bull pens, simple and utilitarian like a Glock. Sarah Underwood was glaring at her computer screen and scribbling notes. Deputy Griffith wasn't in—his turn at the courthouse. Marshal Warren sat quiet in his office, devoted to a report on his desk. The new guy, Howell, Collin Parks' replacement, was with either Griffith or the Chief Deputy somewhere. No prisoners. A quiet room, as Manny liked it.

Noelle Beck wore better clothes these days. The classic blue blazer remained, but it was tailored, and beneath it was a tight scoop-neck black t-shirt, instead of the ill-fitting white button-down. She'd taken to wearing short pendant necklaces, two at a time, miracle of miracles. The first year of their relationship, she'd been a mousy-haired mess with splotchy skin. But now? Now she used night cream and concealer and better hair products, and the whole package made for much better viewing across Manny's desk.

She caught Manny's eye and stood from her desk. Her desk with three monitors, whereas Manny's had one that sometimes he didn't turn on. Together they walked to the far hallway and into a secure room, Beck carrying her laptop. Manny activated the door's electronic access code and opened it for her and they entered the SCIF—Sensitive Compartmented Information Facility, as required by the National Counterintelligence and Security Center—a room only they used. Manny triggered the deadlock bolt, and Noelle connected to the RH-shielded internet access. She satisfied several security measures and the face of their JFIC supervisor popped on screen.

Special Agent Weaver, chief operating officer of the Joint Federal Investigations Commission. A hard woman who could use some night cream.

"Good morning, agents," she said. "You've been activated."

Manny felt a thrill. He'd been busting local thugs for months.

"Yes ma'am." Noelle pushed the screen back an inch so they could see Weaver more clearly.

"I received a call from our contact at the CIA. He has an emerging situation he'd like handled out-of-office and handled quietly. That's why we exist. Can you leave imme-diately?"

Manny nodded and Noelle said, "Yes ma'am, we can."

"I'm not interrupting an imminent wedding ceremony, am I?"

Noelle flushed and smiled and didn't dare glance at Manny.

"No, we haven't set a date."

Manny knew several words existed that sounded the same but had different definitions. Eminent, immanent, imminent, and no matter how hard Mackenzie tried to teach him he would never master them and he didn't know which Weaver intended. Important, maybe?

"Good. I need you on a plane later today," Weaver said.

"Our destination?" said Manny.

"Abu Dhabi."

Manny and Beck were both startled. JFIC was domestic, not international.

"Isn't Abu Dhabi..." Manny waved a hand. "Somewhere else? Far? Where the hell is Abu Dhabi?"

"In the Middle East, on the Arabian Gulf, though some call it the Persian Gulf."

Manny grunted. He didn't know where that was by either name. In Arabia, obviously.

"That's on the other side of the world," said Noelle. "A twelve-hour flight, I'd guess."

On screen, Weaver nodded.

"Fourteen. I wouldn't ask you, but our CIA representative is desperate. He has two teams in the Middle East, but they're engaged, and he wants this done quietly without alerting the local officials and without using military."

"What's the job?" said Manny.

"Bring an expat home."

"Expat means expatriate," said Noelle, correctly guessing it was outside Manny's lexicon.

"Someone not patriotic anymore?" he said.

"No, it's an American living abroad. Apparently this one is important."

"He is," said Weaver. "A non-stop flight leaves from Dulles in four hours. Can you make it?"

Manny grinned. "If we average ninety on the interstates. Other words, we'll get there early."

"Good. Thank you, agents. I know this is last minute and beyond our normal modus operandi. Pack quick and go, and I'll prepare a briefing with further details."

The picture blinked off.

"I'll drive," he said.

Noelle closed the computer. She felt the same thrill as him, though mingled with anxiety over her to-do list she'd be neglecting.

"Where is the Arabian Gulf?" she said.

"You don't know either."

"I know exactly where Abu Dhabi is, and the Arabian Gulf. I'm curious about your geography knowledge."

"In the Middle East. Obviously, Beck," he said.

When Beck smiled wide enough, she had dimples.

"What other countries border the Arabian Gulf?"

"India," he said.

"Not even close."

"China."

"Even worse," she said. "Think of Abu Dhabi like a state inside the UAE." She paused and saw no flicker of awareness. "The United Arab Emirates."

"Who cares. It's outside the US, that's what matters. What kind of extract lives on the Arabian Gulf."

"*Expat*." Noelle triggered the bolt to open the door.

"A bad American, that's what kind." He withdrew his phone and fired an unclassified text to Weaver.

>> First-class seats, jefe. Fourteen hours is a long time.

3

———

After a mad race across Virginia, and flexing their marshal privileges at the airport, Manny and Noelle lifted off inside a Boeing 787 Dreamliner on Etihad Airways, non-stop to the United Arab Emirates, at 1 p.m. They were scheduled to arrive at 10 a.m. Gulf Standard.

First-class was booked solid, but Weaver got them into business. They sat inside their own pod, with a half wall between them that could be raised. Manny had a Bellini after takeoff—very underrated, the peach—and Noelle drank orange juice.

She watched the assignment briefing sent to her iPad by Weaver, listening through headphones. After a second viewing, she passed the device to Manny.

He pressed play and Weaver's voice filled his head.

"Agents, I hope you're enjoying your flight. Try to rest, because the jet lag will get you if you're in-country longer than we anticipate.

"Through a stroke of luck via our government's surveillance efforts in the Middle East, the CIA has learned of a planned attack on William Sloan, an expat living in Abu

Dhabi. Mr. Sloan began his career at Time magazine before helping to start one of the biggest television companies in the US, Lorimar Telepictures. They made *Dallas*, *Knots Landing*, *Thundercats*, *Alf*, and others, and the company was acquired by Warner Bros in the 1980s for a huge sum. He moved on to work as an executive overseas for large companies, including ING Barings. He's a big deal, he's well connected, and a personal friend of multiple high-ranking government officials. He was asked to help Abu Dhabi build a local film and television industry, and within a decade Image Nation won Oscars for *Free Solo* and *The Help*."

On screen was a carousel of William Sloan photographs. Good-looking guy with grey-blonde hair, glasses, and a sly smile. He wore a tie in every photograph.

Weaver continued. "We believe he is simply in the wrong place at the wrong time. An extremist terror group known as the Houthis is spreading in the Middle East, and their contingent in southern Saudi Arabia is looking for an easy American target and decided on William Sloan, one of the highest-ranking Americans in Abu Dhabi. Needless to say, his execution or abduction would be international news, which is surely the intent, though we're not sure why yet.

"Mr. Sloan doesn't know he's been targeted. Intelligence indicates he is to be abducted three days from now by a Houthi strike team."

Manny pressed pause and lifted one headphone.

"What's a Houthi?"

"I'm researching that right now." Beck's phone was connected to the plane's wi-fi. "An Iranian-backed Yemini terrorist group."

"They have their own country? Houthi-stan?"

"No, they operate illegally out of several middle eastern

nations. A close comparison would be Al-Qaeda. Think of the Houthis like..." She clucked her tongue thoughtfully. "Like if the KKK was outlawed but they were backed by Canada to bomb America and Mexico, for the sake of White supremacy. That's the Houthis, but for Shia Islam."

"What's Shia Islam?"

"A division of Islam. I think."

Manny dropped the headphone cushion back around his ear and pressed play.

Weaver continued. "At the request of the CIA, your job is to make contact with Mr. Sloan tomorrow at his home. He lives at the Shangri-La hotel. Obviously this will come as quite a shock to him, and you'll need to diplomatically explain the situation. You're a scalpel, not a hammer. At the end of this briefing is a personal video created by his friends at the CIA, imploring him to leave with you immediately. Escort him to the airport, get him on the plane, and safely return him to the States. The American Embassy in Abu Dhabi has been made aware of the situation, but we want Mr. Sloan out of the country, not merely taken to the embassy. A small UAE anti-terrorist team will meet you at the airport, escort you to the hotel, and then return you to the airport with Mr. Sloan. The CIA believes the Houthi movement has sympathizers inside Abu Dhabi, which means the anti-terrorist team knows only that they are to safely escort you to and from your destination. They will know nothing else.

"As soon as Mr. Sloan is safe, which we assume will be approximately sixteen hours from now, the CIA is prepared to share their intel with Signals, the UAE equivalent, and leave the counter-terrorist response up to them.

"Thank you, agents, for responding so quickly. You're

helping save a man's life and preventing an international incident."

The screen changed to a list of details, including the Shangri-La's address.

Manny handed the iPad back.

"He lives at the Shangri-La hotel and made that movie *Free Solo*? I like this man," said Manny.

"He's quite impressive. That's probably why he was targeted."

"Shangri-La in the United Emirates? I'm surprised. Isn't the UAE a bunch of guys wearing masks with machine guns?" he said.

"That's Pakistan. The UAE is a safe, prosperous place, different from Yemen or Syria, or even Iran."

"All Muslim?"

She winced at him. "I'm not an expert on that. You'll have to ask someone else. I know not all Muslim cultures are the same."

"We're flying fourteen hours there and fourteen hours back for a simple two hour job," he said.

"Somehow, though, it's never simple."

A stewardess arrived to take their dinner order. Manny requested an appetizer of fruit and cheese, followed by the steak and couscous, finishing with the chocolate tart.

"What champagne do you have?" he said.

"Charles Heidsieck, 2006."

"Rosé?"

"No sir, I'm sorry, only the Brut," said the stewardess.

"Keep the Bellinis coming, please."

"And for your wife?"

"She's not mine. She'll be someone else's soon and my new partner will be ugly," said Manny, his mood souring.

Noelle ordered the sweet potato soup, followed by blackened cod and lemon sorbet.

"I'll miss this," said Manny.

"Miss what?" said Noelle.

"This. Us. You ordering the wrong thing."

"I didn't order the wrong thing," she said. "And besides, getting married doesn't mean I'll quit the NSA."

"Of course it does, Beck."

Her mouth dropped a fraction, indignant.

"I'm not marrying him for the money. And I don't want to quit."

"You'll be living in Washington and traveling the world, seeing to his enterprise. Ay, you haven't thought this through." Manny pushed the button for his chair to recline. Three hours separated them from their dinner.

"Maybe he'll move to Roanoke."

Manny declined to comment.

"*Maybe.* He might," she said. "And I'm not sacrificing my career."

"Yes you are, and I hate my new partner already." He closed his eyes and stopped the chair at a forty-five degree angle. The fuselage around them rattled and hummed, bearing them northward along the coast, upward to Canada and then across Greenland.

"You're being ridiculous. We don't even have a date set."

"What about a venue? Or a dress?" he said.

"I suppose you have strong feelings on both?"

"Elope. Somewhere warm. And make the dress short. Your legs are *muy encantadora*. Your best feature." He pushed the button to raise the partition, sealing off Noelle's surprise.

∼

THEIR FLIGHT TOOK them against the sun, and they traveled through an entire night in six hours. The 787 skimmed the northern part of the world before plunging south over Europe and western Asia. They ate and drank well and watched the new Top Gun movie together, the fourth time for Manny. Pete Mitchell, the finest American. They fell asleep with the partition lowered.

When the Dreamliner touched down, it felt like three in the morning for them, but in Abu Dhabi it was nearly lunch. This wouldn't have bothered a younger Manny but he blinked and blearily wondered when he'd gotten old.

They deplaned and a uniformed woman waited in the ramp with a Sinatra sign. She took them away from the other passengers, bypassed security checks, and outside to a motor pool of anti-terrorist police vehicles—Mercedes E-Class sedans. Men wearing tactical gear waited.

Manny and Noelle ducked at the heat.

"*Ay dios,*" said Manny.

The uniformed Arabic woman smiled. "Yes sir. It is 110 degrees Fahrenheit."

Manny slid his sunglasses on—Randolph Engineering aviators, made in America, close enough to Maverick to satisfy him—and Noelle said, "I should have brought a hat."

Manny glanced at the sky, hazy with the noon heat wave.

"This sun, you won't burn, Beck. You'll die."

The woman opened their doors. One of the men wearing tactical gear loaded their luggage—one overnight satchel each. None of the special forces team carried assault rifles. Pistols only.

"Your police drive Mercedes?"

The woman smiled politely without answering.

Manny looked wistfully at the driver's seat but decided

not to ask. Without knowing the rules of the road, or the local customs, better to let someone else steer.

The driver spoke English well enough that his accent required no deciphering. "Where to, sir? Madam?"

"The Shangri-La Hotel. You know it?" Manny was pleased the whole world spoke the King's English. Or the President's English.

"Yes, sir. Thirty minutes."

Their car rolled forward, followed by another anti-terrorist police Mercedes.

The land was as Manny expected. Flat and arid. Dusty with scrubby plants. However, the culture surprised him. He expected poverty and chaos, but Abu Dhabi looked orderly and clean. He thought the women would be covered to their eyes, but they dressed similarly to airport staff in America, though some wore a hijab to cover their hair. Traffic was light as they approached the city from the east.

Manny pointed. "All the big trucks. They're in the right lane."

The cop spoke over his shoulder. "It is the law, sir. Trucks can only travel in the right lane. They cannot even pass."

Manny was stunned. What a great idea. Could Abu Dhabi have a better law than America? Cargo trucks in the right lane only. Brilliant.

Beck indicated tall poles on the side of the road.

"See those? Speed cameras. Smart dynamic traffic monitoring. Abu Dhabi is one of the first cities to use them," she said.

"What do they do?"

"If you're speeding or not wearing your seatbelt, the cameras identify your car and fine you immediately," she said. "Or if you're texting, or even tailgating."

"That," said Manny, "is bullshit."

Parts of the future Manny could do without.

The city revealed itself. Most buildings were three stories or less, but random works of art erupted upwards, towers designed to catch the eye. A master designer seemed evident, laying out the city in such a way to avoid over-crowding and traffic, whereas New York City looked like capitalism—build as much as you can as fast as you can, apologize later if you broke the rules.

"Some of this looks like Dubai," he said.

"Dubai is only a two-hour drive north. They're sister cities," said Noelle. In the rearview, the driver appeared impressed. "In 1950, none of this was here. They discovered their oil then and everything changed."

The driver turned away from the towers and drove along an arm of the gulf that wound around much of Abu Dhabi, creating an island the size of a city. He turned through a gate and drove upward along a shaded path, into paradise.

"We're here," said the driver. "The Shangri-La."

4

Their car purred to the sprawling resort, passing parked Lamborghini and Ferrari sport cars. The hotel's bright superstructure was constructed from luxury sandstone and marble and dark hardwoods, accented by lush green gardens.

"*Santo cielo*. Looks like Aladdin and Jasmin live here, *sí*?"

"It's an oasis inside an oasis." Noelle's breath fogged the glass.

The car parked and attendants opened their doors. Inside the second police car, the two officers kept their windows raised and air-conditioners blasting. Manny told the driver they'd be back within the hour. The force of the sun struck them again and drove them into the Arabian palace's towering doorways. The oversized marble lobby smelled like bergamot and rose. Manny shrugged into his striped, seersucker sports jacket.

A young girl dressed in a sequined gown presented warm hand towels, scented with lavender. The man behind the counter welcomed them to the Shangri-La and Manny said they were meeting a resident, William Sloan.

"Yes sir." The man was darkly handsome with long lashes. "Mr. Sloan is our longest tenured guest. Is he expecting you?"

"It's a surprise. Call him for us."

"May I ask about the nature of your visit?" The attendant's English was perfect, like his manners.

"Tell him it's about the sovereignty of America," said Manny.

The handsome man nodded without understanding and spoke to a young bellhop who darted off into the recesses of the palace. Beyond the reception desk, the Arabian waters glimmered under an arched porch.

"Please." The man held his hand toward a welcome bar. "Refresh yourself from your journey, with complimentary water, or a cocktail of your choice."

Noelle helped herself to water that tasted of limes and cucumbers, and Manny ordered a coffee. The brilliant world was hard on his tired eyes. He ate local dates from the offered bowl and took in his arabesque surroundings, and he noted it would be an enterprising terrorist force who attempted an abduction here. He doubted they'd roll up in a van—too many eyes watched the entrances.

The young bellhop returned to speak with the desk attendant.

"My friends," he said, "Mr. Sloan is reading in the shade by our pool, and beckons you join him. Please, I'll escort you."

He led them over a waterway that ran through the grounds, trafficked by small abra boats for when guests wanted to rest their feet, and to the private pool. Glittering white sand and the blue of the Arabian waters beyond.

William Sloan read on a tablet under the shade of a palm tree, near a gurgling fountain. He wore dark slacks and a short-sleeved linen shirt, and he stood to meet them, and grinned good-naturedly. "This is a surprise. I don't see many American agents here." He spoke with a deep, gravelly voice, and he was taller than Manny.

Manny shook his hand and introduced himself and Noelle.

"Am I in trouble?" asked William like a man who knew he wasn't, and wouldn't worry if he was.

"Almost," said Manny.

"Almost?"

"Mr. Sloan we're here on behalf of the CIA," said Noelle. "Not to alarm you, but we've been sent to bring you home. Today."

"Bring me home today." William's eyebrows rose. "Where is home?"

"The United States."

"I live here." He held his hands out to the hotel. "And my second home is in Paris, with my wife."

"*Ay dios*," said Manny. "You're American. Your home's America."

"Originally. Now I'm..." He smiled. "International."

Manny wanted to ask how much money the guy had, rounded to the nearest billion, but he refrained.

"We're taking you to Washington, DC, sir. I know this is a lot." Noelle produced the iPad and handed it over. "You have powerful friends and they send their greetings. Watch their video and you'll understand."

William Sloan accepted the iPad, still non-plussed, and the three sat. He pressed play and the face of the CIA's director popped onto the screen, a pre-recorded message. He said hello to William and explained the situation.

As William listened, Manny drank coffee and inspected the beach. The Shangri-La hotel was long, disappearing south along the wide waterway separating the mainland from Abu Dhabi Island. Across the channel rose more of the city, including Abu Dhabi's Ritz-Carlton and an enormous Muslim mosque. He pointed it out and Noelle told him it was the Grand Mosque, one of the largest in the world, most of it made from marble and pure gold, paid for by an abundance of oil.

"The world dodged a bullet when oil was found here. The ruling family at the time was wise. The enormous amount of money wasn't put into the hands of a terrorist like Saddam Hussein or Osama Bin Ladin, but a good man who loved his wife and kids and built schools and hospitals. That's why Abu Dhabi prospers, instead of making war. It is a peaceful place," said Noelle.

"How do you know all this, Beck?"

"I read, on the way over, like you were supposed to. And you should refer to me by my codename."

"I forgot what it is," said Manny.

"It's—"

"Rickard. I'll call you Mrs. Rocky Rickard," he said.

Noelle sighed and drank from her water glass.

William Sloan finished the video and handed the iPad back.

"You weren't joking," he said.

"No sir. We have an escort waiting outside and a seat for you on a flight leaving in two hours," said Noelle.

"I have a son in Maryland, and an apartment in New York. I suppose I'll use this as an excuse to visit them both." William smiled sadly and looked across the water. "The UAE knows the Islamic extremists will come for them one day. There's too much hate, not to. I hadn't anticipated I'd be involved, however."

Manny held his hands out to the paradise.

"You live at a hotel, *señor*. Why not a house?"

William smiled. "It's nice, isn't it."

"Costs a fortune, though."

"With the reward points I accrue, my kids can fly anywhere in the world for free and not make a dent." He laughed and placed his hands on his knees and stood with the grunt every man makes after the age of forty-five. "I suppose this isn't up for negotiation."

"No," said Manny.

"Intel believes the Houthi terrorists are scheduled to strike in three days. Or is it two? The time difference got to me." To make her point, Noelle yawned. "While there's no immediate danger, we must go."

"I need to make a thousand phone calls." William scratched at his chin.

"You can make phone calls at the airport and send emails on the plane," said Noelle. "I'll set it up for you."

"Very well. I'll go pack." He pointed to a balcony over their heads on the second floor. "That's me. Give me twenty minutes."

He walked into the hotel and Manny and Noelle sat again, taking in as much golden sunlight and peacock blue as possible before returning to the tube of an airplane.

"Guy lives in a beachfront hotel room in heaven," said Manny. "And jokes about credit card points. You think he's worth a billion dollars? Two billion?"

"I don't know. And I'm not sure I care."

"How much is Rocky worth?"

"Same answer," said Noelle.

"You haven't asked him."

"Correct," she said.

"Liar."

Noelle shrugged. "I haven't."

"You don't care how much your fiancé is worth."

"It's a lot. But I make enough for myself," she said.

"Text him right now."

"Absolutely not."

"Give me your phone," he said.

"Rocky is asleep. It's the middle of the night."

"He's not asleep, Beck. He's out killing his enemies with a tommy gun, like a good gangster."

"Sinatra," she said. "Why don't you want me to get married?"

Manny picked up his coffee mug but it was empty. He scanned the beach for a bar in search of something stronger.

"I don't care if you get married. But not to a guy on your caseload."

"Rocky isn't on anyone's caseload. He's not a fugitive," she said.

"You wanna get married? Go ahead. *Vamos*, Beck. But not Rocky. How about Junior?"

Noelle's legs were crossed and she kicked the dangling foot a little harder.

"You mean Leonard James, Bronwen's partner," she said.

Bronwen and Junior had been the brief but bitter rivals of Manny and Noelle, during a battle across Jamaica. They worked for themselves, as mercenaries, rather than exclusively for a government. Bronwen was the operative, Junior the operator, so to speak, in a similar arrangement as Manny and Noelle. Junior was taken with Noelle—she didn't drink, she was a believer, she had a history of working with advanced weaponry and computers with the Air Force—and for a while their relationship bordered on intimacy.

"*Junior*. Big strong bald guy with muscles. You two keep in touch?"

"We do," said Noelle. "Text and email. The last we spoke, he was somewhere in Europe."

"Have you told Junior about your engagement?"

A pause. "I haven't."

Manny grinned. "You're a mess, Beck."

"I know."

He stood and took her water glass and walked inside. He returned with the glass refilled, and with a rum punch for himself.

"Do you think you'll ever marry, Sinatra?" she said.

"Doubtful."

"Why not?"

"I am ill-suited for it," he said, pleased with the word.

"You are one of the most complete men I know. Your life doesn't lend itself to marriage. And yet..."

"Yet I sleep on Mackenzie's floor."

"And you care for me like we're married," she said.

"Get ahold of yourself, Beck."

"You do. You and I are married in many ways. Except there's no romance or sex."

"*Ay dios.*" He sipped his rum. "*Mujer loca.*"

Theirs was an intimate relationship, where they could sleep in each other's bed, or on each other's floor, and share food and drink and money, but certain probing questions about the affairs of the heart were off limits, except in jest. She asked one of those questions now, often wondered but never vocalized. "What about Bronwen?"

He grunted. "You made me marry someone, I'd pick her."

"But you have no plans to."

"Different worlds. Wouldn't work."

"What if she was willing to move?" said Noelle.

Manny held the rum punch in his fist and he tilted it to

look at the swirling colors inside. He took his time answering.

"I don't know. Be easier if we saw each other."

"When is the last time you did?" said Noelle.

"June."

Noelle's heart twitched. "So recently? I didn't know that. What did you... Where did you..."

"A whirlwind weekend, Beck. She flew into Washington for a thing."

Manny drank the punch and set the glass down and fixed his eyes on a dock down the beach. A private place for the hotel's residents to dock their craft. It looked like a fleet of million-dollar yachts, each gleaming white. Manny didn't covet much in the world, but a yacht would be nice. A two-story boat was mooring, seamen dressed in khaki and jackets were jumping to the pier to secure the boat with rope. A couple greeted them, walking farther down the pier to their own vessel. Wealthy people enjoying their wealthy life. Like Beck would be soon.

Manny didn't begrudge her that. Didn't begrudge her the fortunate turn of events, her prosperous future. She was a catch. No, it was more than that. It was Rocky who had a fortunate turn of events. She was the fortune. And he thought she was wise to accept the offer of a man who loved her.

But not Rocky. Not a criminal.

And possibly not Junior either.

Manny hadn't met the right man yet, for him to give her to.

They were deep in their thoughts when shouts rang out inside the Shangri-La. Shouts in Arabic they didn't understand, but they both recognized the pitch—anger.

Noelle glanced at her watch. "William's been gone longer than twenty minutes."

Manny's eyes were on the dock to the south. On the newly arrived boat, the seamen holding the ropes, like they were waiting.

More shouting inside the hotel lobby.

The hairs on his neck rose.

5

"Got a bad feeling, Beck."

"Me too."

Manny pointed down the beach. "Walk that way. Keep an eye on that boat. I'm going in."

Noelle slid the iPad into her bag, and she slipped the strap over her shoulder. Without a word she stepped onto the brick walkway and strode south, toward the pier.

Manny walked briskly inside. He was grinding his teeth.

The darkly handsome man shouted into his phone, words indecipherable. Manny scanned the lobby and saw nothing alarming. He withdrew his badge and addressed the young bellhop who was hiding behind the counter.

"I'm police. What happened?"

Through the lobby doors, Manny saw people running toward their cars. One of the anti-terrorist officers opened his door, as confused as Manny.

The boy was shivering.

"Talk to me." Manny waved the badge at him. "I'm a good guy."

"I don't know," said the boy. "I don't know, I don't know, *la 'aelam , lakiniy khayifatan.*"

"English! Help me understand."

The handsome man covered the phone's receiver. "He does not speak your language well. Please, you must hide."

"Tell me what happened," said Manny.

"Two of our hotel staff were discovered, sir. Murdered. The boy saw it and said they used a gun that made no noise. Please, take cover."

"I'm police, dammit. Where is William Sloan?"

"I do not know, sir." The man pointed down the hall. "The bodies are there. I don't know who did it. The boy makes no sense. *Sayaarat al'iiseaf.*"

Outside the officers spoke with one another, watching the hotel.

Manny couldn't wait. He needed William. "Where are the stairs?"

The attendant pointed and returned to his phone call. Manny ran to the corner, pushed open a heavy door, and found a wide staircase. He drew the service Glock 27 from under his sports coat, and wound his way to the second floor. Peeked into the hallway—thick carpet, golden vases, ceramic sculptures set on pedestals. Quiet. He ran the hallway to the room he judged William pointed at, and he banged on the door. Banged again, his pulse quickened, the hotel strangely quiet.

Two hotel staff shot with a suppressed weapon minutes after he and Noelle arrived? No coincidence.

He kicked the door—the jamb splintered but held. Another kick, straight leg, all his weight, and the door crashed open. He peeked around the frame, saw no one, entered the room, gun forward.

Empty. In the bedroom, the sheets were tossed. The

nightstand knocked over, the bulb broken. A travel bag discarded on the floor.

No body, no blood.

William Sloan had been abducted.

The Houthis were two days early. They'd waited for him in his hotel room. Dammit, dammit.

Manny threw open the glass door and stepped onto the balcony. *There*, screaming down the beach. A disturbance he couldn't make out.

The boat. The terrorist hadn't rolled up in a van to the front doors; they'd docked at the pier.

Where the hell were the Abu Dhabi anti-terrorist cops? Still deciding what to do?

Sinatra leaped from the second-story balcony. He tucked and rolled into the mossy grass next to the brick walkway, and his phone rang as he stood.

In his ear, "Sinatra, I see him! I see William, he's being loaded into a boat!"

Everything happening too fast. He hung up and sprinted down the walkway, feet flying. He moved against traffic, beachgoers running north, away from something, darting into the hotel. Manny shouting, "Move, move!"

A gun shot. More—a short burst.

Dammit, Beck better be behind cover.

The two-story white yacht was pulling away from the pier in a bubbling roil. The seamen once holding the mooring ropes now stood at the bow with machine guns. AK-47s, by the chatter. They fired again, shooting into the air, shouting things in a foreign language.

Where would they go? Manny didn't know, didn't know the city, wasn't even sure where on the planet he was.

The crack of a pistol. Not far ahead of him.

Beck, firing from behind an overturned table. She shot

again and one of the two gunmen on the bow stiffened and groped at his stomach and dropped his weapon, and he fell backward.

Manny shouted, "Good shot, Beck," and raced by her.

"Get down, Sinatra!" she cried but he was in fifth gear.

Aiming while running was impossible but he did it anyway. *Crackcrackcrack*, three shots, casings falling into the sand. The second gunman dove to the deck for cover, and the yacht roared.

The vessel was a Pershing, 110 feet, rented for an enormous sum from the InterContinental Marina an hour north. New, it cost ten million dollars. Gleaming white, comfortably sleeping ten, and built for speed. The captain sat in the cockpit amidship and he pulled firmly on the throttle, heeling the Pershing in reverse and colliding with the floating wooden walkway. He saw it coming in his camera, didn't care, and his jets threatened to rip the planks from their mooring. His boat scraped hard against the neighboring yacht, a far larger craft, and the fiberglass hull groaned and splintered. But he gained the room he needed, his bow swinging out to the channel.

Manny fired again, now into the Pershing's stern, and he raced onto the concrete peer.

The Pershing's name was visible now—إجازة لك

Underneath the script—*Vacation For You!*

The captain punched the throttle. The rearward momentum was arrested and the bow raised to the sky, the boat's powerful engines churning the water into a cyclone. A gunman wearing a blue *battoulah* mask on the top deck aimed at Manny and fired, but the boat's thrust knocked him off his feet and the burst went wide, thumping into soft sand.

Manny jumped onto the wooden planks, nearly falling as the water rose in a wave. He couldn't catch the Pershing.

A couple had been readying their own craft, more of a luxury fishing boat than a yacht. Half the size of the Pershing, but more horsepower provided by three large outboards. A Jeanneau Leader, meant for a day at sea instead of a longer cruise, a mere one million purchased new. The husband and wife were cowering from the gunfire, below deck, but Manny'd seen them and he ran at their boat, *Leader of the Pack.*

He leaped onto the rocking rear deck and gently the craft nudged away from the pier, already unmoored, and he shouted, "America needs your boat! Jump out *now.*"

Below, the couple didn't dare respond.

The Pershing cleared the pier and the captain fed the engine. Fifteen knots. An enormous boat, twenty, twenty-five knots, into the channel that separated the island of Abu Dhabi from the mainland.

Manny stepped to the controls of the smaller craft and his heart turned cold. A myriad of displays and buttons, and he didn't know how to start the engine.

"Beck!" he shouted. "Let's *go*, Beck!"

She was sprinting up the pier, not far.

"Where," he said. "Where, where the hell is the key."

Off his port bow, the Pershing was gaining distance, taking William Sloan with it.

Beck ran the wooden walkway and jumped onto the boat before it drifted out of range.

"Two people below. Get them out," he said. "Ah-HAH." The key was in the ignition near his knees, attached to a foam bobber. He cranked it and the three outboard motors growled to life. 4.2 liter, three hundred horsepower each, and Manny loved them.

He pushed the throttle forward and they surged and he cut the wheel, crunching against the wooden walkway alongside.

"Dammit, sorry," he told no one.

Below Beck shouted, "They don't speak English!"

"Use your gun! Get them up here!"

Manny turned the *Leader* west into the channel, the ship alive and humming under his feet, and he increased the power. Ahead, across the wide swath of water, was the Ritz-Carlton and the rest of Abu Dhabi. Framed by the skyline, the Pershing was in the channel traveling north. It would be out of sight in sixty seconds.

"Let's go, *vamos!*"

The couple came above deck, hands raised. Absurdly young, Arabic, so beautiful they should be on boat magazines. Beck was pointing her gun at their feet, finger off the trigger.

"Jump off," Manny told them.

They didn't move. Didn't dare move or look away from him.

"Jump!" Manny pointed at the water, now gurgling by at ten knots, but they didn't. Like he spoke a foreign language. He grabbed the man by the shirt and the young couple screamed. Manny hoisted him to the side and shoved, and the man fell backward, headfirst into the chop.

His wife didn't wait. She leaped after him, arms whirling, and vanishing under the surface.

Manny shoved the stick and Beck toppled sideways into the co-pilot's chair.

The race was on.

The *Leader* packed on speed, the three propellors gouging the sea and throwing a majestic spray. Manny picked up the Pershing's wake, the needle passing thirty, thirty-five knots, and climbing.

Noelle pointed to their left, the port side, and she shouted in his ear.

"That's the island of Abu Dhabi! It's enormous. Kind of like New York City, except not a peninsula. He has to go north and then west to get around it, to reach the Gulf!"

Manny nodded. Got it. He pushed his sunglasses harder up the bridge of his nose. His seersucker jacket tried to tear off in the wind.

The channel wasn't trafficked with other craft. Too hot maybe. Some of the boat's exposed surfaces burned Manny's fingers. They sped through the shade of Al Maqta Bridge.

"Call the police?" he said.

"I'm trying!" Noelle laughed, an angry sound. The slipstream tossed her brown hair into her face. "I don't know what 911 is here!"

The chase was aggravating and moving too slow, and Manny felt it between his shoulders. If the terrorists were smart, they'd realize they were caught, dump William Sloan overboard and force Manny to stop to pick him up.

And if they were really smart, they'd shoot him first.

The *Leader*, little by little, gained on the Pershing. The sea was a sheet of brilliance that hurt his eyes, despite the glasses.

They crossed under the Sheikh Zayed Bridge and turned westward into the Khor Al Badhal river, aiming at the freedom of the Gulf but still ten miles distant, separated by the long expanse of the city and a network of sandbars and lesser islands. Here other boats motored between the islands of Sas Al Nakhl and Al Reem and Yas and various marinas. Enormous sports complexes and residential high-rises towered on opposing coasts.

"I'm getting no data," said Noelle. "We're on our own."

Manny nodded, not taking his eyes off the Pershing for fear he might mistake it for one of the other vessels. They were within extreme rifle range and he spotted light winking on his prey's top deck. It could be muzzle flashes or it could be the sun's reflection, he didn't know.

Noelle found a sea map in a compartment and she spread it out, pinning it down against the wind.

"We're..." She squinted at the surrounding world, looking for landmarks. "On our starboard, that's the Aldar building, the blue circle one. Which means we're *here*."

She jabbed at a spot on the map that meant nothing to Manny.

Something thudded against the boat's hull, and a forward seat puckered and ripped. "Stay down. We're being shot at," said Manny. "No. Better idea. Take the wheel and keep your head down."

Without waiting for her, he left the little cockpit and moved backward into the kitchen area. He stepped on top of the dining table and rose into the wind, bracing his chest against the hardtop roof ahead of him.

"Hold her steady," he called to Noelle. Leaning forward, he laid his arms on the hot roof to steady his aim beside the radar, Glock in his fists.

The Pershing didn't want to hold still at the end of his barrel, though they'd gotten closer.

"We're too far!" Noelle held the wheel like an expert. Far easier than flying a plane, which she could do.

"I know."

He fired anyway but the *Leader* hit a trough and bucked and he missed by a hundred feet.

"Beck!"

"*What!*" she shouted. "It's the ocean! There are *waves!*"

A man on the Pershing opened fire. A burst from a machine gun. Two bullets shattered the *Leader's* windscreen, glass tinkling into their wake. Manny jumped down.

"Are you hit?"

"No." Noelle pointed to her left, at the broken pane. "I'm fine."

Spindrift misted their faces now. He took the wheel and throttled down, not daring to get closer. They were outgunned.

"We need help, Beck."

"I know." She consulted the map. Looked up and squinted her eyes, then back to the map.

Ahead of them loomed only land. Channels and passages were hidden until you got close. Unless the Pershing's captain was experienced with the maze, he'd be quickly lost.

Four miles behind them, a helicopter was buzzing the channel near the bridges. The sound was inaudible but Noelle tapped his shoulder.

"The anti-terrorist unit," she said. "That has to be their chopper."

Manny indicated the flotilla of white luxury boats in the Khor Al Baghal, a wide river.

"That chopper can't identify one boat from another. Unless you figure out how to talk to them, Beck, it's no help. They'll never see us. *Maldita sea, estoy tan enojado.*"

The Pershing rounded a point in the labyrinth of islands and cut sharply inland, toward the looming city of Abu Dhabi. She heeled to the starboard, exposing more of her hull. Manny decelerated to thirty-five knots and followed, careful to chase in her wake because he'd noticed parts of these channels were shallow enough that the bottom was visible.

The muscles in his forearms were bunched and knotty. "Where're they going?"

Noelle's fingers traced the map.

"I don't know! They're aimed at something called the Eastern Mangroves."

Across the bow, the big yacht powered its way through the chop toward a sandy shore and low scrubby green plants. A lot of them.

"They're going to run aground," said Manny. "*Ay dios.*"

"They wouldn't. They'll be trapped."

Manny saw it then, their plan. The boat was both their exit strategy and a diversion. Get William Sloan out of his hotel fast via boat, and while the police searched for the yacht among other huge yachts, they'd dump it and take to the streets. All it required was a big deposit for the boat.

And a getaway car waiting.

"They'll run ashore and jump into ground transportation. Get ready, Beck."

"Ready for what?"

"We're doing the same thing." Manny fed more power to his engines. "And we gotta abandon ship quick."

The Pershing closed on the land without slowing. More gunfire from her top deck, not striking the *Leader*. Closer and closer to the vegetation. A collision was unavoidable now.

"Oh cripes," said Noelle.

The Pershing pitched upward, her nose sliding into sand. The captain killed the engines but her momentum carried her far into the mangrove swamp, destroying the undergrowth and splitting apart the field of green. A riot of colorful birds took flight. The boat beached itself, a sudden stop—the frame bent but held, glass shattering forward, water and sand erupting in a plume, and the man Noelle shot earlier was launched from the bow, the momentum cartwheeling him into the trees. The boat settled and canted to the right. Men jumped into the knee-high water and some of them opened fire on the *Leader*.

ThumpThumpThump, into their hull.

"Hang on."

Manny aimed away from the larger yacht, getting distance between themselves and the gunmen. Bullets spouted the water around them and snapped at their ears, and then Manny was plowing into the mangroves, hidden from sight, ugly twisted branches tearing at them. They kissed the shallow sand and suddenly thrust upward, aiming at the sky briefly, the ground acting as a ramp. The boat settled and slammed to a halt—Manny was thrown into the controls and Noelle into the bulkhead. A large bow wave rippled ahead.

"C'mon." He grabbed Noelle's hand and pulled her down the sloping deck. The *Leader's* architecture groaned and complained at being grounded, her keel threatening to break. After the drone of the engine, the silence sounded alien.

They stepped on the gunwale and cast themselves into the water. Not deep but tangled with mangrove roots and Noelle said, "Gross," and Manny agreed.

Gunfire behind them.

Manny threw himself over Noelle and they submerged, but no bullets came for them. Instead gunmen raked the *Leader*, pumping round after round into the fuselage. A terrible sound, the chatter and destruction. A flock of pink flamingos lifted off to escape the noise, crying.

Keeping only their heads above water, they moved

deeper into the mangroves, toward shore. Warm salt water in their mouths, damp organic stench in their noses. Angry calls behind them, and the machine guns silenced.

This was absurd. Yesterday he bought steaks from Fresh Market and they marinated overnight and he planned on grilling them over charcoal and watching a baseball game. Instead he was ducking into a swamp across the world, and how the hell had that happened.

"That," whispered Noelle, "is the biggest turtle I've ever seen."

Manny didn't look.

"Focus, Beck. Don't think about snakes."

"Cripes," she said. "*Cripes cripes cripes.*"

From behind a water-logged bush, a man surprised them. His arm was broken, and he bled from the head and stomach, both crimson and dripping into the sea, the man Noelle had shot, the man launched from the boat's impact. He limped at Manny, teeth clenched, holding a wicked knife in his good hand.

Barely an adult.

He swung at Manny and growled something unintelligible. He missed wide.

Manny stepped in and took the knife away, absurdly easy, and jammed the blade home where the guy's jaw met his throat. A gurgling sound and the man knelt awkwardly, water up to his face—he'd be dead in ten seconds.

Manny hated it.

"Come on." He held out his hand to Noelle.

The earth was rising as they neared the shore and Manny saw light ahead. They pulled each other dripping out of the Arabian waters and onto the sandy tidal flat, to the edge of the scrubby mangrove plants. Manny tore off his jacket and hurled it angrily into a bush. A road lay before them, and they took cover behind a sand hill—one hundred yards northward, two vehicles waited. One like a moving van, and the other a pickup.

"My shoes cost two hundred dollars," said Manny. "So did that jacket. And your pants are new. Someone owes us."

"How'd you know my pants are new?"

"Be serious, Beck."

The city of Abu Dhabi rose ahead—the skyline was broken between conventional three-story buildings, arabesque works of art, and glimmering towers, far as the eye could see. They'd never find William Sloan in that urban jungle.

A gang of men ran from the shrubs, dripping and dirty. Eight total. One man held his stomach and hobbled, and another pushed William forward with an assault rifle, shouting at him. Two of them looked like boys, and they all wore old sports jackets and head coverings, strangely formal. Over their shoulders were slung weapons and satchels and canteens.

"I'm getting on the rear truck," whispered Manny. "You reach a main road and flag down a car or taxi or something, and call for help."

"Roger."

"*Roger.*" Manny made a disgusted face. "You don't say Roger."

"I wanted to try it."

"Never again, Beck."

The gang loaded the trucks, four into each. William was hoisted into the cargo van, and the door rolled down, and his captors boarded the cab. Manny ran at the cargo truck, his shoes squishing. He ran unobserved until the last man dropped something and stepped out of the cab for it. He saw Manny and jumped backward into the open door.

"*Mrhban , hunak shakhs ma huna!*"

Manny cursed, drew, and fired—that was his fifth round —and caught the man in the face, crimson spattering the window.

More shouting, "*Antalaq , antalaq , antalaq , asrie!*"

The first truck, an old red Ford Ranger, gunned its engine and tires spit gravel. The cargo truck snarled and lumbered forward, leaving behind the fallen terrorist. The cargo bay rocked back and forth on the service road, the side door open and banging.

Manny caught the dusty cargo truck easily and hoisted himself aboard, with a dim memory of doing the same thing once in Jamaica. The convoy sped down the road alongside the glittering sea, leaving the mangrove swamp. Noelle left her hiding spot and ran perpendicular to the service road, leaping a barrier to reach the nearby highway. He'd be out of her sight soon, Manny knew, and he hoped she could track his phone.

If the sea hadn't ruined it.

The trucks passed a gorgeous waterfront palace—did everyone have those?—and merged onto Highway 10. At the first intersection, the trucks turned into Al Fahd Street. The water was left behind as they motored into the heart of Abu Dhabi, intending to get lost.

Manny knelt as best he could and worked the rolling door but it was locked. William was inside and Manny shouted at him.

A dirty sedan pulled out of a villa and trailed the trucks. Then another car behind it.

Manny waved at the two men in the sedan. "Aye! Hey!" He mimicked a phone with his free hand. "Aye! Call the police! You know police? Help!" he shouted.

Instead, the passenger produced a rifle and rolled his window down.

Of course.

Manny dug into his shoulder holster and ripped free the Glock as the man leaned from the window and thrust the rifle out.

Manny fired twice—*six, seven*—both bullets puncturing the windshield and drilling the gunman. The driver swerved and braked, tires squealing. Three bullets left. One day he'd upgrade his pistol. He liked the 27 because it was small, but the 41 held three extra rounds. Bigger ammo too, which would be nice.

Think about that later, Manuel, aye, estúpido!

The car behind the sedan, an old dirty coupe, raced onto the curb to clear the sedan, and sped after the truck. The passenger stuck a pistol out the window and fired wild, missing the cargo truck entirely.

Manny took aim. The coupe was too far. He fired anyway and missed—*two* rounds left. He couldn't reload with a single hand, but if he let go of the cargo truck's handle he'd fall.

The convoy motored through an intersection, cars honking angrily. A motorcycle raced the other direction. nearly colliding with the stalled sedan.

Another car, a Mitsubishi Pajero, appeared.

The Mitsubishi had taken lead of the convoy at the Al Fahd intersection, but now decelerated to the rear. The Mitsubishi traveled beside the cargo truck, not four feet from Manny. The driver's window buzzed down and he shouted. He fumbled for something on the passenger seat, grabbed a black pistol, and aimed at Manny at a distance he wouldn't miss.

Everyone's a terrorist here!

The distant coupe fired again, bullets smacking the cargo door near Manny's head.

The whole world shooting at him, he was out of options, out of time. At forty miles per hour, he jumped from his perch on the truck bumper and landed on the hood of the Mitsubishi. The driver fired at him in midair air and missed. Manny and the driver stared at one another through the windshield, the man dark and mustached— there was no passenger—and he mashed his brakes. Manny's left hand was curled under the gap where the hood met the wind-shield and he held, otherwise the inertia would've flung him toward the front bumper and the rushing road. His wet shoes slipped and he landed hard on the hood, but still his maintained his grip.

Ay dios, the hood was *hot* and burned his hand.

With his other hand, he pressed the Glock directly into the glass and fired—*nine*. The bullet splintered the glass and missed its target, but shards sprayed into the driver's eyes.

"Ya lilqarafi!"

The Mitsubishi swerved and squealed. The car fishtailed and lost its speed and Manny was slung to the side. He hit the ground at ten miles per hour, and rolled with it, and came up kneeling and knew his joints would hurt later. The Mitsubishi hit the curb and stopped, and its driver spilled out of the door, cradling his face and shouting.

The dirty coupe halted in a squeal of rubber and two men stepped out, one armed with a pistol, the other an AK-47, and they hid behind their open doors. Manny possessed no cover and one bullet. The cargo truck was pulling away, already two blocks distant. Things not looking good.

Manny raised his hands and stood and said, "Don't shoot." He needed something—cover, another gun, the Mitsubishi, something, anything. The men laughed and shouted words he didn't know and they were going to kill him.

Dive for the Mitsubishi and pray, he thought, but it was too far, and he was a dead man.

Then there was the motorcycle.

The same one from earlier, a gorgeous red and black Ducati. The helmeted driver locked his front brakes, and spun in a circle, rear wheel screaming and smoking behind the gunmen. The professional maneuver brought the motorcycle even with the coupe's rear bumper, and he brandished an automatic pistol; the gunmen were stunned stupid. Two shots, *crackcrack*, and two more, *crackcrack*, and the gunmen fell, choking and grabbing their chests.

The driver holstered the gun, and Manny admired his style.

He lowered his hands.

"*Gracias.*" He wiped his forehead and took two deep breaths. "Or however you say that in your language."

The motorcyclist nodded, the visor reflecting a sparkle of sunlight. He revved the engine and released the front brake. He popped a wheelie and roared after the retreating cargo trucks. Chasing the Houthis too? Who the hell was he?

Manny stepped to the Mitsubishi's door, kicked the blinded driver in the stomach and told him to stay down and not fire his gun at Americans, and ejected the magazine. Plucked another from his belt, slammed it home, and released the slide.

He tucked behind the wheel and closed the door and shifted into drive. The engine rattled and growled, and he resented the motorcycle its speed. Seven blocks ahead, he could still make out the cargo truck, and the Ducati gaining ground.

His foot mashed to the floor and the car whined forward. He gripped the wheel and flexed every muscle in his body, furious.

"*Aye, dammit, why am I in the Middle East getting shot at? Odio este lugar!*"

And where the devil was Beck?

The Mitsubishi was packing on speed and racing past honking cars, Manny's left hand on the wheel, the right holding his Glock, wishing he had another hand for his phone, peering through clear spots in the fractured windshield.

The bike raced through the Al Yassiyah intersection, and the terrorist's red Ford Ranger charged from its hiding spot. An ambush. The truck had pulled over when they weren't looking, and now it clipped the rear tire of the Ducati. The bike spun and laid over, spinning across the blacktop. Sparks flew, more honking. The motorcyclist let go and went into a controlled slide, as racers knew how to do, feet first, bracing himself with his hands, and collided with the far curb, helmet clunking off the road.

Four men poured from the red pickup. All of them with assault rifles, and Manny was *sick* of those.

They advanced on the motorcyclist, firing as he dove behind a cluster of date trees, bright bursts and fresh wood splinters. One of the four gunmen turned and saw the Mitsubishi a split second before Manny ran him over. The car mowed down three of the men, sick thumps—one guy under the tires, another crashing into the windshield, another smashed against the front bumper, and Manny drove straight into the side of the Ford Ranger, killing the man, and the airbag deployed in Manny's face.

He shot the bag—*one*—to deflate it and climbed out, his car coughing and dying. One terrorist was left standing in the intersection, stupefied at the Mitsubishi and the driver, not knowing where to turn, and the motorcyclist shot him once, and the assault rifle clattered to the ground.

The terrorist who'd bounced off Manny's windshield groaned and fumbled with his gun and Manny killed him and finally the world quieted, other than the ringing in his ears.

Terrorists neutralized.

The cargo truck was gone. *Gone* gone. So was William Sloan.

Manny smacked dirt from his ripped pants. His shirt was damp and caked with dust, and he was scraped and cut everywhere. The motorcyclist limped from behind the little grove of date trees. Manny pulled the phone from his left pocket—four missed calls from Noelle.

He didn't aim his gun at the motorcyclist but he didn't put it away either. The man was an ally.

Hopefully an ally.

"You and me look like we're on the same team, *amigo*," he said. "Though I don't know how to say that in Arabic."

The motorcyclist looked up from his fallen bike. Tilted his head. He unlatched the chinstrap and pushed the helmet off his head.

Blonde hair the color of afternoon sunlight spilled out, and Manny was looking into the big green eyes of Bronwen Davies, the girl who visited his better dreams.

"Sinatra, my darling." She smiled. "I seem to be following you around the world again. Lucky for both of us."

6

The Capital Gate hotel was shaped like a twisting tube of glass, situated on the southern side of the island of Abu Dhabi. Manny sat next to Bronwen on the eighteenth floor lounge, outside, a glass of tequila and lime in his hand. Before him, the city spread like a blanket of Christmas lights, distant towers twinkling at the northern beaches. Even at eight in the evening, the temperature hovered over ninety degrees, but it was breezy and tolerable.

Despite the shock at seeing Bronwen, there had been little time for talking—midtown was in an uproar. The Abu Dhabi Mobile Data Transfer System was bringing in unmarked squad cars from all directions. She exfiltrated him on the back of her bike, away from the scene of the battle, away from incoming police, returning him to the Shangri-La. She kissed him hard there, and arranged to meet at Capital Gate later. He rendezvoused with Noelle and they made contact with the American Embassy before the Deputy of Criminal Investigations could put their faces on the news channels; Weaver was attempting to reach Major General Faris Khalaf Al Mazrouei to quash the Abu Dhabi

Police's manhunt. Manny booked them a room at Capital Gate, ordered a driver to take them to a clothing shop, and then to their hotel, running on no sleep.

Now, hours after the gun battle, Bronwen sat next to him and Manny found himself sitting straighter in his chair. She was shorter than him by two inches but he needed erect posture to maintain it. He wore khakis and a white linen shirt purchased at the nearby boutique, plus new Lucchese boots. He was bruised and scraped head to toe, but the tequila helped.

Across the table, Leonard James Jr. had his arm around Noelle, their faces aglow from the candles on the table.

Manny wasn't happy about the arm.

Noelle updated them—stopping the wheels of the manhunt would take time, so they had to lay low; the whereabouts of William Sloan remained a mystery; police found the empty cargo van, but no terrorists—the strike team had ditched it and taken shelter, probably in a predetermined apartment in the city, waiting for the right moment to drive to Saudi Arabia.

Noelle hadn't disclosed to their supervisor the arrival of Bronwen and Junior. But she would. Soon. Possibly.

Manny indicated the city. "I like this place. Like some of America's better parts were dropped in the Middle East."

"And some of England," said Bronwen. "An Emirate is like a monarchy, you know."

"Are you Bronwen? Or are you Alice Worsley?" he asked, referring to both her given name and her alias.

"Junior and I are on a job." She reached across to push a strand of hair out of Manny's eyes. "So I'm Bronwen. Though you may call me what you like."

"You're not here on behalf of England?" said Noelle.

"Nah, we tried that life. A whole year. But we got bored

as hell. Too many rules, not enough money." Junior squeezed her hand again. He was a big strong man, Black, shaved head, and a long-time partner of Bronwen's on clandestine assignments. He hadn't released her hand yet and Manny was resisting the urge to bring up her engagement. "We're taking jobs again, you understand me."

"Who's your current client?" said Manny.

"A wealthy conglomerate with a vested interest in oil production. A terrorist is making their lives harder, interfering with operations and reminding the world they should invest more in cleaner energy. The deal is under the table." Bronwen only had eyes for Manny, like a theatergoer viewing her favorite play.

She was strong and rangy, and she wore a top that crisscrossed and exposed her midriff and other curves, and her cheeks pinked each time Manny noticed. Emerald stud earrings matched her eyes and the dainty pendant necklace.

"What's the assignment?" said Noelle.

"Zayn Abdul Aziz. A brilliant Middle Eastern leader making war against the Sunnis, the dominant ethnicity in Saudi Arabia. Zaz, he's called, in the international community," said Bronwen.

"I know Zaz." Noelle brightened. "Know *of* him. He's a Houthi terrorist."

Bronwen waggled her hand. "He's a terrorist, that's true, but he's only *hiring* himself out to the Houthis. His religion is money. Right now, the Houthis are paying him the most, so for the moment he's an Islamic revolutionary. Next year, who knows."

"Not if we kill him first," said Junior. "He's our target. Man making all kinds of trouble."

"Your mission is to assassinate him?"

"Find him. Call it in. Give the go-ahead for a strike. That

fails?" Junior shrugged a meaty shoulder. "Yeah. We kill him."

"And he's in Abu Dhabi?" Noelle asked.

"Not sure. He was outside Al-Obailah, a settlement in the southern Saudi deserts, but we caught wind he was doing something in the UAE. Here," said Junior.

Noelle and Manny made eye contact.

Could it be a coincidence?

Although their mission was classified, they'd already shared some of it. JFIC existed to handle problems quietly, and that required discretion and rule-bending.

"The Houthis are here for William Sloan, an American *expatriate* leading Image Nation, an Abu Dhabi film and television company. We came to extract him, but the Houthis got him first." He paused, pleased with expatriate and extract. "They struck ahead of schedule, and we don't know what they want with him. Soon as we get better intel, we'll attempt a rescue."

"Then our purposes align, loves. We both benefit from Zayn Abdul Aziz's head on a plate," Bronwen said.

"I want William Sloan. You can have the head," said Manny.

"Is there anything else you want?"

An unmanly knot rose in Manny's throat. He wanted this woman. Yet he said, "Some sleep."

"I can think of something more restorative than that, Sinatra."

Manny checked his watch. It was 9 p.m. in Abu Dhabi. What time was it in Virginia? He had no idea. Nor did he remember the last time he slept.

"Let's pool resources. *Comprende?* We hear something, we tell you. You hear something, you tell us. About William

Sloan or Zayn Zaz or whatever the hell it is. We do this right, we all win. *Sí?*"

"Sounds alright to me," said Junior.

Bronwen nodded at Manny. "Whatever you say, darling."

He took her hand and pulled her up. "Then you and me are taking a walk."

"Absolutely we are."

Manny led her through the doors into the cool of the eighteenth-floor lobby. On his way out, he heard Noelle say, "Junior. We should talk about something," and the doors closed.

"You're more beautiful than I remember, Sinatra. Or would you prefer Manuel?" said Bronwen.

He caught their reflection in a mirror next to the elevator bank. He looked exhausted. She looked like the cover of a magazine.

This woman.

Most men were intimidated by her. She glowed with fitness and strength and noble breeding. She strode the earth like an Olympian, like a boxer, like a fitness instructor, like she'd been designed for him.

The only makeup she wore was mascara. She wore no lipstick and no blush, and nothing underneath the criss-crossed blouse.

He pulled her into the elevator and the doors closed. He had a room on the twenty-fifth floor. Hers was on the twenty-second. Neither pressed a button. They stood in the corner like floating, his arms around her, her face pressed against his neck.

When she spoke, her lips brushed his collar bone.

"I missed you."

"I missed you," he said.

"The worst part is picturing all the women who fancy you. Who get to live on your street."

He took some of her hair into his fingers. The deeper strands were still damp from her shower. Only so many natural blondes existed; most women faked it.

She pulled away. "Manny, my love. Alice Worsley has many suitors. She's minor nobility, after all."

"Not so minor in my eyes."

"She's a hot commodity. But she rejects them all." She pressed a button, the twenty-fifth floor, and the elevator surged upward. Then she untied the knot of her blouse. The two crisscrossing folds over her chest loosened and fell to her side, exposing her to the navel. "Did you know, darling, I haven't touched a man other than you since we first met."

"Haven't you." He reached for her.

"So you understand," she said and she pulled the blouse completely off, "if I'm eager to spoil you tonight."

7

———

The sun punched through the gauzy curtains too early. Far earlier than it ever did in America, land of the place where things made sense.

Manny woke missing his country but the sense of longing faded at the sight of the woman next to him, sheets kicked down to her waist. He forced himself out of bed and briefly considered taking a photo of Bronwen in her sleep, but he was no voyeur. Or at least he wouldn't document proof of it.

He examined himself in the mirror. His shoulder and thigh were darkly bruised from falling off the Mitsubishi. He'd left patches of skin from his palms and forearms on the street. His chest was tender from slamming into the speedboat's control panel.

Worth the sacrifice, for the sake of last night.

He twisted the shower on hot and stepped inside, and the steam soothed his aching joints. A scar along his spine had tightened during the night, but the heat eased it. He worked his left foot up and down, a morning routine to alleviate pain from an old injury, and he shaved his face and neck, and he leaned back against the cool shower wall and closed his eyes and pushed wet hair out of his eyes. His body reminded him he shouldn't be waking up; he should be falling asleep, Virginia time. Bronwen opened the door and joined him, and the shower lengthened to thirty minutes, filled with fog and whispers and desire. There was no duty to king and country, no pain, no past or future. When finally Manny turned off the spray, they realized someone was knocking at the door.

Manny answered it in a towel.

The woman there resembled Penélope Cruz, he thought, the actress from the good horse movie. Like most women in Abu Dhabi, she was trim and dark-haired with long lashes, and for a treasonous moment he wondered if there was more natural beauty here than America.

They clearly ate fewer Big Macs.

She took in his chest and wet hair, and she offered an apologetic smile. "Good morning, Mr. Sinatra."

"Just Sinatra. Good morning."

"I am Liya," she said. "Liya Al Ariani, analyst with Signals, the UAE's intelligence agency. Would you join us for breakfast, please." She glanced at his tattoos, forbidden in Islam, and down to the towel. "Your colleague Ms. Beck is already there."

"IF WILLIAM SLOAN IS HURT," said Manny, his fist gripping a hot mug of coffee, "I'm holding this whole country responsible."

He addressed Yusuf Torres, a hard man in a police uniform. What little hair he had remaining was buzzed to the scalp. Yusuf was chief of the Police Special Unit, Abu

Dhabi's counter-terrorist group, modeled after the British SAS. It had been his team sitting inside their cars as Manny and Noelle chased their ward into the Arabian Gulf.

"You are a fool." Yusuf's English was good. "A fool if you think weak threats will get him back."

Behind Yusuf stood Liya Al Ariani, the woman who'd fetched Manny. Next to Manny sat Noelle Beck, drinking tea, all of them in a secluded nook of the hotel's restaurant. They each had coffee and a plate of sausage and danishes. Just visible through the glass door, Bronwen and Junior ate on the outside patio.

"Tell me this. Why do you Muslims hate each other? Why would a Muslim group come into a Muslim country and kidnap an American to make other Muslims look bad?" said Manny. "The whole world wants to know the answer to this question, by the way. Not just me."

"Bah." Yusuf waved a hand. "You are too disrespectful, and I will not answer. I could not answer, as I was raised in the Philippines, and came to Abu Dhabi as a police recruit, and don't understand the sects myself."

Liya Al Ariani looked pained by the question. "In Abu Dhabi, we know we face an uphill climb, in terms of global relations. We know the world sees Muslim garb and assumes terrorism. And we fight hard against it. Abu Dhabi is one of the safest places in the world. It's true, look it up. We work hard to make it so."

"That doesn't answer my question."

"Although the United Arab Emirates is more inclusive than the rest of the Arabic world, we are predominately Sunni. The Houthi Movement is a branch of Shia."

Manny spread his hands, like—*Which means?*

Liya smiled politely at the handsome American. "It dates back to the founding of Islam and disagreement about the successor to the prophet Muhammad. I can bore you with names and traditions you don't understand. When Muhammad passed, the *Ummah* was split about whether Abu Bakr or Abī ibn Tāil should lead, which resulted in the First *Fitna*—"

"Ay, hell no," said Manny.

"I thought as much. The easiest way to summarize it—while both are Islam, the Sunnis and Shias fight like hateful siblings."

"Different denominations who can't get along."

"Yes." Liya squinted and searched her memory of Christianity. "Think of it like Protestants and Catholics."

"Except we don't kill each other."

"Not recently," she said, and Manny conceded the point. "The UAE is a nation of peace, and predominately Sunni. The Houthis are violent terrorists, and Shia extremists. They hate us. And they hate America too."

Manny ate some of the sausage on his plate. Whoever the hell Sunnis were, they made terrible sausage.

"Do you remember Ibolya Ryan?" said Yusuf.

"No," said Manny.

"Yes." Noelle set down the tea and wiped her mouth with a napkin. "She was an American murdered in Abu Dhabi."

"An American teacher, living here. In 2014, she was stabbed to death inside a mall. The killer was a Muslim woman wearing a veiled niqāb. International news. She was a lone wolf killer, but still the world associated the violence with Islam, making global relations more difficult. Tourism suffered. So you can see," said Yusuf and he jabbed the table with his finger, "why your street fight yesterday is so damaging to us."

"Have you wondered why William was abducted two days early?" said Manny.

"You had bad intelligence. You should have trusted us to get him out immediately," Yusuf barked.

"Wrong. There's a Houthi traitor in your ranks. Our government called you, and the traitor sped up the abduction. We shouldn't have trusted you *at all*. There's no street fight if you have no Houthi traitor working for the Abu Dhabi government."

"Finish your breakfast." Yusuf's face was dark with displeasure. "Drive to your American embassy. Leave this to us."

"I'm getting William Sloan back."

"You're a fish out of water, American. You cannot help," said Yusuf. "We'll find him."

"How will you?" said Noelle.

"We have a, ah, *jasus*, inside the Houthi ranks." Liya still stood behind Yusuf, as though she needed his permission to sit. "A spy. I believe you say, a mole? We have activated the spy, or mole. He should tell us the Houthi's plan with Mr. Sloan."

"And you'll share it with us?" said Noelle.

Liya smiled at Noelle with less warmth than she had Manny. "Most likely, my supervisors will share with your supervisors."

"If Mr. Sloan is still in Abu Dhabi, he is my responsibility." Yusuf stood, forcing Liya backward. "And the responsibility of our people. If he passes outside our borders, we will defer to you. Until then, return to your embassy. Or better yet, get on a plane. A police escort is below, ready to help you leave. I must return to work." He made a little bow and walked toward the exit.

Liya Al Ariani watched him go before leaning closer to Manny and Noelle.

"I am sorry for him. He is police. I am intelligence. We often work together but..." She shrugged apologetically. "Sometimes it is better if we leave police out of things until we need them?" She set a business card on the table and pushed it forward. "I will let you know if I hear anything. And you please do the same? *In sha'Allah.*"

She turned and hurried to the elevator.

8

Manny and Noelle continued their breakfast without speaking. Both were tired and frustrated. Manny returned to the buffet for fruit, which he reasoned couldn't be prepared poorly, and more coffee. He also resorted to eating bread.

"Are we going to the embassy?" asked Noelle.

"Be serious, Beck."

"I didn't think we were." She smiled into her mug.

Bronwen had finished eating and she reclined in her chair, face tilted upward to the sun behind oversized sunglasses. Manny enjoyed this from a distance. Beside her, Junior spoke into his phone.

Manny nodded at Junior. "What'd you tell him?"

"Who?" said Noelle.

"Junior. You know what I mean."

Noelle quietly searched the table for answers to the mess she found herself in.

"I told Junior the truth. Rocky asked me to marry him and I said yes."

"How'd he take it?"

"He..." Noelle picked up the tea. Paused. Set it down again. "He has concerns."

"Smart man."

"Oh hush."

"Tell me this, Beck. If Junior asked first, would you now be engaged to him?"

Noelle made a groaning noise. "I will not answer that."

"What if I asked first?"

"Then I would assume you had a concussion."

"Did you sleep in Junior's room last night?"

"Of course not."

"Did you go there at all?" said Manny.

"*No.*"

"Did he come to yours?"

"I'm not playing this game." She walked outside to the patio and she sat beside Junior. Manny asked the bartender for a mimosa and he joined them a moment later.

Ay, the heat.

"What'd that angry dude tell you?" asked Junior.

"To stop shooting up his city and get the hell out. *Está lleno de mierda.*"

"They don't know where your guy is."

"No they don't," said Noelle.

Her face still tilted upward, Bronwen took Manny's hand. "Your trip's gone pear-shaped, hasn't it, darling. Other than us."

"Manuel. My man. You know about this Rocky thing?" said Junior. "The *proposal*?"

Manny grinned.

"I heard."

"And you didn't tell me?"

"Thought you'd like to hear it from Beck herself," said Manny.

"She was hiding it from me, cause she knows it ain't right."

"She's a mess. Doesn't know what she wants. I have to pick out her clothes."

"Boys," said Bronwen. "Be nice. She's a big girl. She can play with whatever toy she wants."

"She wants my toy. That man, he ain't even a professing Christian, you know that?" said Junior.

Manny drained his flute and set it down. "What is he? A satanist?"

Noelle sighed. "I'm not discussing this."

"He's agnostic," said Junior.

"That's like when you can't smell?"

"Means he don't know and he don't care about God."

"Beck, *caramba*. You can't take a gnostic home to your Mormon mother."

"*Agnostic*," said Noelle. "And we're... We're working through our belief systems."

"Trouble is, she can't take a Black man home either," said Junior.

"That's not true!"

"No? Let's try it."

"I'm engaged! To someone who isn't you."

"Yeah but you ain't happy about it. Let me meet the folks," said Junior.

Manny grinned.

"I want to be there for it, *por favor*."

"Okay." Bronwen forced herself to sit upright in the chair. "Okay, enough of the silly. What's your plan, Sinatra? Are you fleeing the country?"

"The devil we are."

"You do have a plan?"

"Of course I do. I'm American."

"Mind sharing it with me?" said Noelle.

"We're returning to the boat crash."

Noelle made a hmm'ing noise. "That's a good idea."

"Obviously."

Junior waggled his phone. "Just hung up with a local guy. Our boy Zaz is in town. Spotted in the hotel district. We gone meet up to discuss."

"The Houthis hired him to abduct Sloan. But why?"

"We don't know that for sure."

"It can't be a coincidence he's here," said Noelle.

"Imma squeeze our contact for anything he knows. Might get us closer. We can't call in a strike on Abu Dhabi soil, though," said Junior.

"Well then." Bronwen stood. "Let's be off. The day awaits. We have terrorists to silence and hostages to rescue and all that, don't we? And then perhaps another night here at the hotel?"

Her sunglasses flashed with the sun, like a wink at Manny.

"We'd be stupid, otherwise," he said. "Lady Liberty and England should encourage their diplomatic relationships."

"I already canceled my room," said Junior. "Be alright I sleep with you? Like last night?"

Noelle stood, her face red and angry. She pointed at Manny. "I don't want to hear it. He slept on the couch."

"Things were getting good, too."

"*No* they weren't. They were..." Noelle threw up her hands. "They were complicated." She stormed into the hotel.

Bronwen kissed Manny on the cheek.

"Careful today, love. Don't sacrifice yourself. A world without Sinatra sounds dreadful."

"Doesn't it," he said.

A POLICE CAR loitered in the hotel's roundabout, ready to take them to the embassy or, preferably, the airport. Instead, Manny and Noelle slipped on sunglasses and hid their faces from cameras, Noelle inside a hijab, Manny ducking under a hat. They walked through the rear service exit and down the stairs. Unseen by the police, they retreated a block in the angry heat and waved down a cab. Manny asked to be taken to a car rental.

The driver held up his hands.

"*Madha? La 'afhamu. English no, English no.Ana la atahadith alankiliziata.*"

Manny ground his teeth.

"Car rental. Hertz? Avis? Enterprise?" said Noelle.

"Ah!" His face widened into a smile. "Enterprise. Enterprise car."

They were whisked ten minutes to a familiar bright green storefront, a comforting sight. Manny produced the JFIC credit card and his international driver's license, which listed his name as Sinatra.

The clerk's English was passable but required multiple attempts.

"The nicest car you have," said Manny.

"Yes sir. Nice car." The man clicked his mouse and peered into the screen. "A big car, sir?"

Manny pointed over the man's shoulder to the outside lot beyond and a glittering red car waiting there, ready to leap.

"Is that a Maserati?" said Manny.

"Yes! Yes sir. Maserati Ghibil."

"Sinatra, you cannot be serious." But Noelle was grinning.

"Like hell I'm not."

Ten minutes later Manny was behind the wheel, Beck beside him, punching up a map. While not one of the luxury Maserati models, the Ghibli was a well-muscled sports car. Sleek and low to the ground, five hundred horsepower, a simple interior but designed to please the eye. If only it'd been a stick shift.

Less bulky than the Camaro. A higher seat, more windows, easier to see the world. He liked it.

"Nothing but the best for you, Beck."

"May I drive it?" she said.

Manny gripped the wheel and wished he wore leather driving gloves. "Break up with Rocky and I'll consider. Tell me where to go."

"Left. And keep in mind, these roads might have sensors that monitor your speed."

"America can afford a traffic ticket." Manny left the parking lot in a roar of rubber and fuel, the engine surging without effort.

As they drove, Noelle gave him a brief history of Abu Dhabi. The magnificent city through which they drove did not exist seventy years ago; compared to an ancient metropolis like London or Athens, Abu Dhabi was still in infancy. Their culture was built on exporting pearls, dates, and coffee until approximately the 1940s, when Japan learned to create beautiful artificial pearls, crippling their economy. Finally the leadership of Abu Dhabi signed oil exploration agreements. Drilling began with modest results, until the 1950s when larger and larger oil fields were discovered, both offshore and inland. The Sheikh was delivered an infinite amount of wealth. More money than he could ever spend. He was a good man with a vision for the future, and he invested in infrastructure and schools and hospitals, not a war machine. The city thrived. The leadership of Abu Dhabi was conservative, and remained so today; however, they began broadening their vision. They wanted a culture and economy founded on more than hydrocarbon wealth. They spent billions on tourism—towers and beaches and exhibits like a Louvre, a Formula 1 racetrack, palaces, Ferrari World, the Grand Mosque, extreme sports, luxury restaurants. They built beyond what their tourism traffic required, instead seeing a future where the hotels would be full. The city was prepared for the crowds that arrived in greater droves each year.

"That's why the city isn't congested like New York or Los Angeles. Abu Dhabi planned ahead," said Noelle.

"It's good to be rich." Manny caressed the Maserati's wheel.

"It's good to be wise."

"How do you know the history?"

"I read it last night," she said.

"After you finished with Junior."

"Sinatra, don't be crass. Nothing happened."

Manny heard the truth of her words, and he also heard truths underneath them she hoped would remain secret.

"I saw you holding hands, Beck. You may not have slept with him, but you're more than friends."

"That is not your business."

"Is it Rocky's business?" said Manny.

"Why are you asking! You don't care about Rocky."

"I care about you," he said, and Noelle didn't respond. "I care about loyalty and fidelity and trust. I say that right, fidelity? You're a good person, Beck. The best person. But not if you start betraying yourself."

Manny didn't know the speed limit. His race car was smoothly passing every vehicle in sight, tickets be damned.

"Sinatra," she said. "Manny…"

"I'm listening."

"It's complicated."

"Loyalty isn't complicated."

"It's because you made me wear makeup," she shouted, suddenly irritated. "It's because you talked about my legs and abs and I should show them off, and use better conditioner and buy face cream, and wear heels and low-cut shirts! Boys I admired didn't admire me back! I was a computer geek. And now, cripes, I don't know what to do. High school was no crucible for rejecting boys, I wasn't trained."

"You told a man you'd marry him."

"I really like him." Noelle spoke the words to Manny, to herself, to the world. Spoke them like an incantation that could magically fix things.

"And Junior."

She leaned her head against the window. "I know."

"Deep down, Beck. Under the garbage and the words. What do you want?"

"I want you to go slower," she said.

"I'm serious."

"I don't know what I want, Sinatra. *Clearly*. I'm torn."

"Tough spot for Rocky to be in."

"Do you know why I said yes? To Rocky? Because that's what *you* do. That's what Mackenzie does, and Veronica, and Stackhouse. You pick a direction and you go. You go and you *make* it the right direction as you're going."

Manny pressed his teeth together and clenched.

"I'm not wrong, am I?" said Noelle. "So that's what I did. I made a decision. Am I in love with him? Probably not. Do I feel like he's *the one*, like in romantic movies? Probably not. After we make vows on the altar, *then* he'll be the one.

Because I'll have promised it. Decisions and discipline are more important than emotions. I learned that from you, Manny."

Manny nodded. Heard himself in her words.

"I made a decision. It's a good decision. I'm working on the discipline. I'm ignoring... I'm *trying* to ignore conflicting emotions. And it's the best I can do," she said.

Ahead of them, the glittering Arabian sea rounded into view.

"Okay. *Bien*. I get it, Beck. I get it." He took a deep breath, didn't know what else he wanted to say, and let the air out with nothing behind them.

"You get it."

"I think so."

"You don't. Sometimes I believe you understand nothing about me," said Noelle.

He looked at her and she didn't meet his eyes. She was attractive, even on the job in the Middle East. A few years ago, she looked like a mousy computer nerd, thin and pale and insecure. Now she was stronger, more full of life and confidence. Her chin held higher.

"Good for you, Beck."

"Good for me."

"You look sexy shouting. Good for you, telling me to shut up and mind my own business. And I will."

Noelle's chest rose and fell with unspoken thoughts.

"That man you make a promise to at the altar," he said. "Ay. Rocky or Junior or someone else, he's getting the girl of his dreams."

"Mmhm."

Northern Abu Dhabi was bordered by two mangrove swamps. Manny had crashed his boat into the smaller of the two. Upon return, they discovered the service road blocked off by a white Department of Transport truck. Manny waved his badge at the man and he motored around the truck without stopping to discuss it. Two miles down the road they passed two Criminal Investigations Directorate cars, an unmarked car, and another white truck. Visible over the scrubby plants were two UAE Coast Guard Al-Saber patrol boats and one tug, bobbing at anchor a quarter-mile offshore.

Manny drove beyond the vacant police cars to the sand dune he and Noelle hid behind yesterday. He kept the car running for the sake of the air conditioning.

"I'm going in. You stay here and if anyone asks, wave your credentials. They push you, call the pretty girl."

"Bronwen," said Noelle. "She can't help."

"No, the Muslim intelligence girl. Lyla. The one with the lashes."

"Liya Al Ariani. She did have great lashes. And I can handle this."

Across the barricade, cars raced by on the highway, oblivious to them. They raced by in an orderly fashion, not daring to break the law.

He and Noelle were alone—the occupants of the nearby cars in the mangroves, searching the grounded boats for evidence. He kicked off his leather shoes. Unbuttoned his shirt and stepped out of his pants, down to his boxers.

"You do have a specific goal, I assume?" she said.

"I get in there, Beck, I'm taking off the shorts. I refuse to get more good clothes wet. Don't watch, otherwise you'll be sad for other men."

"I've seen you naked before, Sinatra. In prison, remember."

"I get better with time."

Manny walked across the scalding gravel to the tidal

flats, into the warm sand and water. The lapping surf reached his knees after thirty paces. He steadied himself by holding onto a stalky tree he couldn't name, and he carefully lifted each foot out of the boxer shorts, and left the garment dangling from a branch before walking deeper into the swamp.

Noelle watched this, a smile on her face and a pressure swelling in her chest.

There were no men like Manny Martinez.

He lowered until his chin touched the water and he moved deeper, almost invisible. The swamp swarmed with pungent life. The birds and turtles didn't seem to mind him, and he refused to consider other animals.

Through the flora he caught distant flashes of his boat, which was closer than the larger yacht. He heard men calling to each other in Arabic, and a man inside a kayak was trolling the shallows.

Manny grew disoriented in the maze and had to approach his boat to get his bearings. The search party was focused on the larger yacht, allowing Manny to move unseen in the murk. From the boat, he slowly worked his way back toward Noelle, searching the floor of the mire. He travelled too far, and he cursed, turned around, and walked it again. The hunt lasted twenty minutes but he found his quarry.

The man he killed with a knife.

Still here, undiscovered three feet underwater, surrounded by a myriad of minute fish. Manny hauled the corpse up and foisted him into the crook of a tree trunk. The corpse's flesh was protected from sunlight by the salt water, but swollen and grey.

Manny turned in a circle, searching the dank forest; he was alone. In the man's pants pockets Manny found a set of keys. In the jacket, a sodden copy of the Quran and unreadable papers. A satchel was tangled around the guy's neck and shoulders; Manny yanked the knife from the corpse's throat—a nice knife, Persian, engraved upswept blade—and cut the strap, freeing the satchel. Inside, Manny struck gold.

A water-proof phone. He slipped the knife into the satchel, zipped it, lowered into the water up to his chin, and waded his way to shore.

He walked naked as the air out of the water, reclaimed his boxer shorts, and stepped carefully over the gravel back to the car.

He opened the rear door and slid in. "I'll dress after I dry off. No more damp clothes, Beck."

"Being nude in public might be a capital offense in a conservative society like this," she said.

"They're jealous." He handed her the satchel and she lowered her window and held it outside so it wouldn't drip on her. "Found it."

She unzipped the back and withdrew the phone.

"What made you think to look?"

"America is my muse," he said. "We get lucky, there'll be Houthi correspondence on there."

She turned the device over in her hand. "It looks new. Probably waterproof. I'm unfamiliar with the Huawei brand. We'll need to buy the right charger."

"Wish I'd brought a towel. I'll be dry in five minutes."

She half-glanced at him over her shoulder and smiled.

"Take your time, Sinatra."

9

They found a phone store inside the Galleria shopping mall. Four levels of shops—Abercrombie & Fitch, Gucci, The Gap, Cheesecake Factory, Texas Roadhouse, Bath & Body Works, American consumerism, plus luxury shops he'd never heard of—bright with light and smiling employees, but mostly empty. Manny asked the salesman why, and he explained it was too hot, that shoppers would come out that evening, far into the night.

He and Noelle bought coffee from a Starbucks—Starbucks was ubiquitous and uniform—and took over a large table in the corner. She charged the Huawei phone from her laptop until it blinked on, and she smiled.

"We've got power."

She unlocked the phone with an NSA program and used her finger to swipe through the apps.

"It would be handy," she said, "if one of us read Arabic. I assume this is Arabic."

As she scrolled, the phone received a backlog of messages and emails, undecipherable by either of them. The letters looked like scrawl.

"What time is it in America?"

"Which time zone?" she said.

"The best one."

On cue, Noelle yawned. "Close to midnight."

"You're hungry. I'll get you food."

"Thank you. I'm calling Weaver to get help with Arabic." Noelle dialed a number on her own device.

Manny wandered the lower floor of the mall and ordered two salads from Joga. As they prepared the food, he stepped into Gucci. He browsed the mismatched, ugly, poorly designed, floppy outfits, clearly intended for an insecure blind creature addicted to heroin and social media, and decided society might be doomed. He was no French sissy but he did find gorgeous low-cut sneakers and a white pair of cotton joggers. And *this* raffia bucket hat would look spectacular on Noelle.

When he returned with a Gucci bag and two salads, she was speaking with someone in her earpiece and peering intently into her computer screen. He ate half his salad, laid prone on the bench, and fell asleep immediately.

When he woke, his feet were in Bronwen's lap.

"Look what I found at the shopping centre." She squeezed his ankle. "A fit homeless man."

Across the table, Junior and Noelle were discussing something technical that his foggy brain didn't catch.

He sat up and rubbed his eyes.

"Good morning," he said.

"Good afternoon, love."

"Tell me what you learned."

"Our informant is a contact who works for Abu Dhabi's version of Skynet. Their facial recognition software picked up Zaz's face in the hotel district. He refused to discuss it over the blower, so we met face-to-face."

"The hell," said Manny, "is a blower?"

Bronwen grinned. "Blower. Slang for a phone."

"Why do you call it that?"

"I've no idea, really. Silly, aren't we. Anyway, our contact showed us the photos. It's him, Zayn Abdul Aziz." She handed Manny two glossy photos of a man riding in the passenger seat of a car. A striking man in a blue suit. Strong jaw, dark eyes, short salt and pepper hair. "Handsome, isn't he, this terrorist."

"He looks rich."

"He's got millions in the bank. But he wants millions more," said Bronwen.

Manny rubbed his eyes and yawned. "By being a mercenary. Hiring out to terrorists."

"Our Defense Intelligence believes Zaz was behind the recent coup in Yemen, and last year's riots in Egypt."

"Now he's kidnapped an American in Abu Dhabi. To do what?" said Manny.

"Assuming it was him. We still aren't positive."

Manny found his cold coffee and drank deeply from it.

"Tell me something good, Beck."

She took out her earpiece. Junior kept doing something on his phone.

"I'm screen-sharing with an Arabic analyst in Washington. We believe the phone belonged to an insurgent named Hashem. The man you killed. Hashem is still receiving texts and emails, but they're in a crude code. They say six o'clock but they mean three. They say north, but they mean west, that kind of thing. Our Arabic interpreter says the code is not sophisticated but it'll take time. Junior's using his own code-breaking software. What is clear is that William Sloan isn't their only target."

"Who else?"

"We don't know."

Their foursome and the gadgetry on the table was getting curious looks from the passing shoppers.

"We should send the Houthis a text. Ask where they are," said Manny.

Noelle nodded. "That's what we're working on. However, we think they'll smell a rat."

"This is what we got." Junior cleared his throat. "Brothers, I'm alive. Hurt but well, Allah be praised. My phone was ruined. I bought another. Send me the address."

Manny nodded. "Makes sense."

"You'll text it to the group?" asked Bronwen.

"In Arabic. That's the plan."

"What if you singled out Hashem's closest friend?" she said. "It might feel more genuine, that way."

Noelle and Junior both pursed their lips thoughtfully, gazing at their phones, and Manny rolled his eyes at the synchronicity.

Nerds.

"That would be Abdo," said Noelle. "They have a close bond. We think."

"Still though." Junior shook his big bald head. "It doesn't feel authentic to me. Like Hashem should say something more specific to the Houthi cause."

Manny's gaze fell on the satchel. From it he removed the Persian knife. Wickedly sharp, the blade curved. He ran his fingers over the engraving. Two lines of little words that ran the length of the steel.

"Beck." He set the knife on the table and slid it across. "Have your boy interpret these words."

Noelle took a photo of the blade and texted it to her Washington contact. A moment later she read, "It means,

God is the Greatest, Death to America, Death to Israel, Cursed Be the Jews, Victory to Islam."

"A pleasant bunch, aren't they, these Houthis," said Bronwen. "What's wrong with Jews?"

"They killed Jesus," said Manny. "You can't do that."

Noelle read off her screen. "Apparently this is a common Houthi slogan."

"Use it," said Manny. "Send the text, but include Victory to Islam."

"Good," said Junior, typing. "That's good. Victory to Islam."

"Wait." Manny raised his hand, gears in his mind churning. "What's his name, Abu? In the message, request he call us."

"Abdo. But we don't speak Arabic," said Junior.

"If he calls, can you use the connection to pinpoint his location? Using towers or whatever geek stuff you have?"

Junior and Noelle glanced at each other, pursing their lips again, and the synchronicity aggravated Manny.

"Probably," said Noelle. "But then Abdo would know he's been had when Hashem doesn't answer."

"Have your Washington interpreter answer. Act like the connection's bad, but keep him on the line. We only need a minute, *sí?*"

"It could work. *Could* work."

"We find Abdo, we might find William."

Junior resumed typing on his phone. "How about this. 'Brother Abdo. I'm alive, Allah be praised. Hurt but well. My phone was ruined. I bought another. Call me with the address. Victory to Islam.'"

"I'll talk it through with our interpreter."

Manny stood to pace while Noelle and Junior spoke to Washington.

Bronwen joined him and they let their technicians work without interruption, and they strolled deeper into the multicolored mall without speaking until passing a baby clothing store.

"Do you want children, Sinatra?"

"I have one," said Manny.

"You do not."

"I live in the house with a boy named Kix. He's... I don't know. Five? How old are kids when they learn to walk?"

Bronwen laughed. "Younger than five. Older than one. But he's not yours."

"He's as close as I want to get, *señorita*."

"I cannot imagine having a child. Wouldn't we be horrid parents?"

"He'd be the toughest kid at school, though." Manny grinned at the thought.

"Or she."

"I can only make boys."

She nudged him with her elbow. "You'd be aces with a little girl, Sinatra. I'm weak-kneed at the thought of you parenting."

Manny was struck by a pang of homesickness. An empty feeling in his chest, across the world in a mall. A welling of all the things he didn't have, that the job cost him, that life decided he'd never experience. Like a wife. He stopped and gathered Bronwen to him and held her, and the hurt was halved.

She spoke into his shoulder. "Are you okay, darling?"

Shoppers slowed to watch them. Was an American movie being filmed here? Who were these two gorgeous people?

"Not that I mind the cuddle, but are you alright? Manny?"

He released her.

"It's the time difference." He faked a smile. "It makes me soft."

"I was worried you were about to propose."

"Worried? Other women would kill for it," he said.

She laughed. "Don't get me wrong, love. I just meant, not in a godawful shopping centre. There's at least a bit of romance left in my body."

He pulled her to a bench and they sat and he wrapped his arm around her shoulders and they watched a family order cookies at a bakery.

"What do you want, Bronwen. From life."

"My, aren't we thinking deep thoughts. The same things you want, I expect. To serve my country, the scenery to be ever changing, to be free, to have adventures, to crawl into bed with a gorgeous spy as often as I can," she said. "To *go*, to *live*, and do it well and fast."

Manny nodded. Those were goals he could endorse.

"What do you want, Sinatra?"

"Similar," he said. "Though, we want those things for different reasons."

"I kicked against stuffy aristocracy since I was a little girl. You can't imagine the paddlings I endured, rebelling against my parents' sacred cows. I despised the tea parties and manners and fake smiles, so I escaped into the world. I like my family where they are—in one place where I can pop in as I like."

In other words, she was running from her past.

Manny was running toward his future. He was using freedom and adventure to create a life, not to shake one off.

"We're running in opposite directions," he said.

"Are we?"

"Do you think we could live together?"

"Of course, though we'd be flatmates who never saw the other," she said. "Always on the go."

"And if we married?"

She shrugged. "Sinatra. I'm head over heels for you. Do you know it? But neither of us would quit our career, would we? We're too…"

"Broken."

"And destined to die young," said Bronwen.

"Ay, likely."

"Would your mate Mackenzie let me live there?"

Manny let his head tilt upward and he grinned at the distant ceiling. "Be a full house."

"And we'd have to sleep on his floor, wouldn't we."

"Depends on the night."

"Either way, Sinatra," she said, and he lowered to face her and she kissed his lower lip. "Either way, married or not, floor or not, since I met you, one thing is obvious. I'm yours."

NOELLE HELD her breath and pressed send on Hashem's phone, texting their message to Abdo.

The four of them stared at the device, plugged into both Junior's and Noelle's computers, as though it would ring immediately.

Which is what it did.

The screen lit and the ringer chimed.

"Damn that was fast," said Junior.

"It's a different number." Noelle read the screen. "This isn't Abdo. Or he's calling from another line. Ready?"

Manny and Bronwen nodded.

Noelle pressed a button on her computer. The call was

picked up and intercepted by a program allowing the Washington interpreter to speak.

Immediately Junior's computer began a digital search for CSLI information from nearby cell towers. Numbers flashed on his screen and a map sprang into view.

The man from Washington answered with an improvised static background.

"*Alhamd allah 'akhi. 'atamanaa 'an takun jid.*"

None of them understood it, partly because it was Arabic, and partly because the words were broken, a ruse to disguise the interpreter's voice.

"*Alhamd allah 'akhi. 'ayn 'anti?*" said the caller.

"*Ma zilt fi 'abu zabi. alhamqaa 'aslahuu lay. ladaya dhirae maksur. 'ayn 'anti?*"

Back and forth.

They listened for half a minute as the men spoke, the line growing increasingly distorted, and Junior raised his fist. "I got him. His exact location. An apartment south of here."

Noelle touched a key on her computer and the call ended.

She immediately sent a pre-determined text to Abdo in Arabic.

>> **Bad signal. I will contact you again.**

"He's still in Abu Dhabi," said Junior. On screen, a blue dot blinked on a map.

Noelle put her call with Washington on speaker. The interpreter said, "That was not Abdo. Abdo is dead. Whoever he was, he is disappointed Hashem didn't have the good sense to die for Islam. But he said tonight is still happening. I don't know what it means, though. He asked Hashem to meet them there."

"Where?" said Bronwen.

"I'm not sure. He assumed Hashem knew."

"That means we get to that blue dot. Fast." Manny nodded at Junior's screen. "We find them, we follow them to the next target, and to William Sloan."

"And to Zaz, and we kill that good-looking sumbitch," said Junior.

"We gotta move. *Vamos.*"

Noelle thanked the interpreter and disconnected, and she packed her hardware.

"We have motorcycles," said Bronwen. "Need a lift?"

Manny's blood was pumping. "Motorcycles in this heat? We aren't savages, we have a Maserati. And air conditioning. Race you there, *amigita.*"

10

———

The blue dot was located in the eastern-most apartment of the Arabian Villas, adjacent to the Mushriff Wedding Hall, a set of arabesque tents. This part of the city wasn't designed to delight tourists—the structures were squat and undecorated, designed to look like the brown sandstone fortresses of ancient Abu Dhabi. Manny parked on the far side of the wedding hall, east of the Villas. Bronwen and Junior parked north and south, hidden from sight but with views of the apartment's exits.

Manny's phone told him it was three in the afternoon. His body explained that was false.

The women working under the tents wore full Muslim garb, covering all but their hands and a small circle of their face. They ignored the Maserati.

"They gotta be roasting," said Manny.

"It's their choice. In Abu Dhabi, there is no strict dress code for women. Well... It's their choice unless they married a strict conservative man, but it's not common."

At five o'clock, four men hurried from the rear door of the apartment and ducked into a dusty sedan, which quickly reversed out of the parking spot. Manny wondered how many members of the team remained. They'd eliminated ten, by his count.

Ten. He should get a raise.

Manny fell in behind the sedan, a Nissan Altima. They turned northward on Sheikh Rashin Bin Street and Manny dropped back, giving them space, and then he diverted onto a side road, his spot taken by Junior on a motorcycle. Bronwen raced ahead, ready to track the Nissan from a lead position, everything choreographed over the phone. To avoid being spotted, they rotated through their positions every few minutes until they reached the E12 bridge, crossing to the large Saadiyat Island, half as big as Abu Dhabi proper.

A moving van rendezvoused with the Nissan. Possibly the same van as yesterday—could it be only yesterday?—with different plates. Manny allowed four cars to merge between him and the van as they drove through the marina district.

Noelle plotted their route on her map and she announced, "I think they're driving to New York University."

"Wrong map, Beck."

"It's not. NYU has a campus here." She clicked and read. "NYU Abu Dhabi is a small, private liberal arts school, opened in 2008. The acceptance rate is below ten percent, making it one of the more selective, elite schools in the world."

Manny noted the university on his horizon, rising from the sand as a desert oasis. Dusk was setting in the east and the university lights glowed like a beacon. Like everything in Abu Dhabi, the campus was constructed for the future, rather than the moment, fully formed and pristine its first year. As though designed by Disney or Las Vegas, an exhibit of what a small college should look like, given billions to spend. It was entirely self-contained, set apart from the rest of the city, the distance like a moat of wasteland. There was one way into NYU Abu Dhabi and one way out—the busy Laffan Street, winding its way to the campus from the main city.

In Manny's ear, Bronwen told the group, "I'm already at the campus. There's an underground garage. I'm going in." Manny still trailed the moving van, Bronwen ahead of the convoy. "The parking garage, it's *enormous*," she said and her voice crackled into static and her line disconnected.

"She's underground. We'll be out of contact with her," said Noelle and Manny nodded. Noelle typed on her laptop, examining a map. "The garage is as big as the campus above it. That's incredible. There are three entrances."

"Junior, you follow the van. I'll take up position near the school's exit. They can't leave without me seeing."

Junior copied.

Manny pulled over and parked illegally at a bus stop, and they watched the Nissan, the moving van, and the motorcycle descend the ramp into the underground lot, below the glowing school.

Across from them rose a statuesque structure labeled A1 Building, teeming with student life.

"Junior?" Noelle looked through the windshield at nothing. "Junior, did we lose you?"

No response.

She released a blast of air.

"We should have stopped that van, not let it go underground. "

"We don't have the manpower. And we need William Sloan alive," said Manny.

"You don't think he's in the van? Or the trunk of the Nissan?"

"By now he's been taken somewhere else, not left unattended in a trunk he could escape. Or be cooked to death," said Manny.

She tapped the window with a fingernail. "I wonder how many American students are here."

"Or American professors."

Noelle opened her door. "I'll walk around and see if I pick up their cell phones."

"Don't go far. Maintain visual with me."

"You bet." Noelle walked into the common area beside AI, near a busy sushi shop.

Manny craned his neck to look into the campus. He hadn't been to college and still wouldn't if he could do his life over again. It seemed like jumping through hoops to him, writing papers about plants for professors who would never know him. Anything he wanted to understand, he could read in books, which is what he did.

These kids looked soft. Waiting in line to buy expensive raw fish, staring into phones, taking on student debt and hoping to get jobs without experience. No thank you. Better to live.

He smiled.

Live fast and well.

The Maserati's passenger door opened and a women slid in next to him. Not Noelle.

Liya Al Ariani, the dark-haired intelligence analyst from Signals. The one with long lashes. She wore a pink linen shirt that looked good against her skin.

"I thought I would see you again, Mr. Sinatra. Or, I hoped I would."

"Just Sinatra," he said.

"You didn't call me. I told you we could work together." She smiled and he had the unexpected notion she would look great with a small silver nose stud.

"You didn't call me either. Yet we're both here. Both keeping secrets."

"I followed you," she said.

"I'd have noticed."

"Fine, I admit it. We intercepted transmissions that indicated an attack. We chose not to tell you; it wasn't my decision. Still I find you here."

"Who is we?" he said.

"Our intelligence community. Who, in turn, alerted the anti-terrorism team."

"The ugly bald man," said Manny.

Liya laughed. "Yusuf Torres, the special unit's chief. He is here too. Somewhere, waiting. He does not like you."

"He's jealous."

"I do not understand the connection."

"Forget it. Your English is excellent."

"It's spoken here by most, and I studied foreign languages in Egypt," she said. "I am fluent in Arabic, English, Turkish, Persian, and Kurdish."

She was turned fully toward him, smiling, her hand on his seat back. Like a woman who knew men liked her appearance and she was giving Manny everything she had.

"I'm surprised Islamic women can wear a pink shirt with that many buttons undone."

She looked down. "I am more, um, aggressive than most women here. I wish you trusted me, Sinatra."

"I trust very few, *señorita*."

"Clearly I don't know as much as you. Tell me what you have."

"We don't know the target," he said.

"How did you arrive here, then?"

"Were you born in the UAE, Liya?"

"I was. In Al Whathba, not far," she said. "And you? You don't look like most Americans."

"I'm not like most Americans."

She touched his arm with her fingers. Traced the line of a tattoo.

"Did these hurt?"

"You get used to it."

"I don't think the human body should be marked so," she said.

"Why's that?"

"If Allah wanted, we would be born with them," she said.

"I'm Catholic. We're free will people, not pre-destined." Manny frowned. "I think."

"I don't understand." Still she traced lines on his arm, up to his bicep. "You don't believe in destiny?"

"I write it as I go."

"You are a dangerous man, Sinatra. Aren't you."

He didn't answer. He turned away to find Noelle, who stood near a bookstore, hand to her ear. Liya trafficked in intelligence and she wanted more, and she was trying to get it from him, and he refused to play, no matter how good she smelled.

"What kind of attack do you expect?" he said.

"An abduction. Not an assassination. We hope. And you?"

"My guess is an American professor."

"That is ours too. We have officers inside the faculty residences."

Manny made a sucking sound at his teeth.

"I want to follow the terrorists. Not arrest them."

Liya looked surprised. "How will you follow them if you don't know who they are?"

"What do you mean?"

"You sound as though you wish to let their target be abducted?" she said.

"Unconventional, but yes. Allow the abduction and follow them to William Sloan."

Manny was pleased with unconventional.

"But how will you follow them?" She held her hand to the traffic. "A dozen cars have passed us. Could they be in one?"

A quick recalculation between Manny's ears.

Liya didn't know about the Nissan or the moving van. She didn't know about Bronwen and Junior. He'd assumed she knew. Hadn't her team noticed the big van arrive? They were idiots if they hadn't.

The rear door opened and Noelle climbed in again.

"I can't get anything," she said. "Hello again, Liya Al Ariani. I bet we're in trouble."

Liya looked displeased at the intrusion. "Not if we cooperate. What do you mean, you can't get anything?"

Manny answered over Noelle and he tapped his earpiece.

"Beck and I aren't getting a good cell signal. That's how we communicate, when she and I are separated."

Noelle looked between the two. "Yes."

"Sinatra won't share his secrets," said Liya. "Not even with his ally."

"Get used to it. He'll tell you little of what really matters."

"What's it like," asked Liya, "working with a man like Sinatra?"

"Like solving a puzzle with missing pieces. A puzzle that shouts insults about your shoes."

"Are you his, what's the word, not servant, but assistant?" asked Liya.

"He wishes."

"We're equals," Manny answered.

Noelle cocked her head. "Are we? Can I drive?"

"We're almost equals."

"You're not married," said Liya.

"No," they answered together.

"Do you have sex?"

"*No*," said Beck.

Liya smiled at Manny. "It would be good."

"It would ruin her for every man after," he said

"*Every* man after. How many do you think I'll have?"

"You're very pretty," said Liya. "In Islam, sex is prohibited before marriage. As is homosexuality. Of course, that makes it part of the, um, allure."

"Hah." Manny grinned. "Same in Mormonism. You two have a lot to talk about."

"I don't know why you're smiling, Sinatra. It's the same in Catholicism. Wait until you're married," said Noelle.

"Ay, no one wants to marry me. I should become a monk, Beck?"

"I'll marry you, Sinatra." Liya set her hand on Manny's arm again. "If you promise to share secrets. Starting now."

"You," said Manny, "are sitting in her seat."

A crackle in his ear.

"*Hello*, come in, Sinatra, Noelle, we're on the move!"

Bronwen's voice.

Noelle caught Manny's eye and she tapped her earpiece twice, thump thump, and Manny nodded.

A motorcycle zipped from the far garage exit and turned toward the Maserati.

"What is it?" Liya searched their faces. "What do you see? I'll alert my team."

Manny eased away from the curb and made an illegal U-turn at a To-Go Market.

"In position," he said.

From his earpiece, "They took someone. A Caucasian male. Sedated or drugged, looked like, rolled into the back of that van. I'll get ahead of them."

The black and red Ducati sped past, engine purring, weaving through the sparse traffic; Bronwen left the college campus via Laffan Street.

"Is that," said Liya, watching the bike. "Is that the motorcycle from yesterday's street battle? We caught some of it on camera."

From underground, out rumbled the moving van, closely tailed by the dusty Nissan. Both flicked on their headlights and motored by the Maserati at a respectable speed. Men in the windows stared ahead.

Not Zaz.

"We have eyes on them," said Noelle.

"What? The van? Is that them? How do you know?"

Manny let them drive a block before leaving his spot to take up casual pursuit. He was forced to stop or hit a gang of kids on their phones in the crosswalk and he cursed.

"You're following the van. I'll remain with you," said Liya. "I'll coordinate with our police unit."

"Not necessary," said Manny. " In fact, I discourage it."

"Sinatra, I must." Liya was already typing on her phone. "I have a duty to my country. And you two alone cannot possibly take on a Houthi terrorist team." She stopped texting and glanced through the window, searching. "*Ana mutahamis*. Exactly how many more of you are there? Who were you communicating with? The motorcycle?"

"Ay, pretty *señoritas* always talk too much." The Maserati surged, chasing down the terrorist convoy.

"*That's* what it's like working with him," said Noelle.

In his ear, Junior spoke. "Yo, I'm out the garage, behind you, Sinatra. Imma hang back cause couple of the dudes were giving me looks."

"*Bien.*"

They reached Sheikh Khalifa Bin Zayed Street and merged onto the busy highway. Traveling back toward the towering lights of Abu Dhabi.

Liya's phone rang and she winced.

"*Awh la.* I will be yelled at." She answered and listened and said, "Yes, I'm in the car with the American agents. We are following a van from the university garage. I don't know what's inside."

A man's voice was barking from her phone.

She listened and nodded and switched to Arabic.

"*Naeam ana asfu. ana sawf 'uealimuk bikuli jadidin.*"

She lowered the device and covered the receiver.

"What model car do you drive? A BMW?"

"Maserati. You're in trouble, aren't you." Manny grinned.

"I failed to tell them where I was."

"There's hope for you yet, Liya."

"And he's threatening to send officers to arrest you," she said.

"It'll take all of them."

She spoke into the phone, a growling, aggressive language. Sharp syllables.

"*Nahn narkab sayaarat Mizarati.*"

Noelle maintained a quiet update through her earpiece, helping Bronwen choose her route and remain ahead.

Bronwen had the hardest job, *tailing* the terrorists by traveling in front, but it was an effective failsafe if Manny was stopped.

Manny inched closer to the van, so he wouldn't confuse its brake lights with the galaxy of others, funneling onto Sheikh Khalifa Bridge.

"Back to the city we go," said Noelle.

Liya hung up, pale.

"Captain Yusuf Torres is behind us in an unmarked car. There's another car too, the rest he left at the university. He does not know what to think. He is quite angry."

"*Estoy frustrado con este hombre.*"

"I do not speak Spanish. What does it mean?" said Liya.

"Means your boss better watch his tone with me."

"He is not my boss. It is unusual for a Signals analyst to travel with an anti-terrorist team. But, he is my superior in ways hard to explain."

Manny yawned. He'd be waking up about now, in Virginia. When had he grown so soft. One reason he slept on the floor and drank black coffee and exercised and maintained a strict diet was to remain hard, physically and mentally. Yet here he was, succumbing to a little jet lag.

Despite himself, he felt a prick of relief at the presence of Yusuf and his team. Rescuing William Sloan would be easier with greater manpower.

The Nissan led them across Abu Dhabi, cutting south through the tourist district. Never veering from Zayed The First Street, stubbornly waiting through the string of traffic lights. This part of the city should be buzzing with energy, with people from around the world excited to spend money in the fabled Abu Dhabi, but it wasn't. Scattered persons moved along the sidewalks, but no crowds. The university had been far busier than the tourist district.

"Where is everyone," Manny asked.

"It is the offseason. The sand is too hot to enjoy," said Liya. "This part of the city is for beachgoers. But beachgoers do not arrive for several months."

The Maserati's dash read 101 Fahrenheit.

From any point in Abu Dhabi, certain towers were visible. They rose three times higher than the rest, as though ordinances allowed only a few truly gigantic spires. It was toward a cluster of these towers that they drove.

Liya's phone rang again and she spoke a language unknowable. In the back seat, Noelle was updating Special Agent Weaver. Talking, talking, and Manny tired and irritable.

The Nissan and moving van turned onto King Abdullah Bin Abdulaziz Al Saud Street, and at last into the Conrad Abu Dhabi Etihad Towers. A soaring silver hotel with few cars in the vast lot. Manny watched them from the traffic light.

"The Etihad Towers," said Noelle.

"I'm already parked out of sight," said Bronwen. "But I see them."

Junior crackled, "I'm half a mile back."

The Conrad Abu Dhabi Etihad hotel was a cluster of towers, arranged like God's fingers reaching up from the ground. A resort with enough room for thousands, yet fewer than a hundred cars were parked in the large lots. The Nissan drove to the side of the enormous tower cluster, near a service area of loading doors, far from the glamorous front. Four men jumped out and ran to a closed garage. They weren't dressed as terrorists, thought Manny, whatever that meant. The tallest door was activated and it rumbled into the ceiling, and the moving van navigated into the big space, and the door trundled down again.

Gone.

Manny parked and gazed upward at the lights blinking at the looming peaks, nearly lost in the hazy sky.

"A surprising spot for a hideout," murmured Beck.

Behind them braked the car of an angry special police chief.

11

In the far parking lots of the celebrated hotel, an uneasy negotiation convened within the confines of a barricade formed by the Maserati and two unmarked special police cruisers. It was late and humid and tempers ran hot.

Chief Yusuf Torres was irate. At everything and everyone and he let them hear it. Intelligence analyst Liya Al Ariani should never have been brought along, his superiors be damned. She had left her post, disobeyed direct orders—treasonous—and was too friendly with the American agents, who would be deported on the first plane possible. Or, if he had his way, handcuffed and deposited into the overcrowded Sweihan Prison.

What the hell was on that truck? Did they know conclusively? Could they be chasing an innocent moving van, helping college kids transfer luggage from the hotel to the college and back?

Analyst Liya, renowned for her insight into the extremist Muslim terror groups, had few answers. She claimed the American agents seemed to be cooperating with other entities, but she didn't know who or where. Nor what brought them to the university.

Most of this was communicated in Arabic.

Worst for Yusuf, the American agents paid no heed to his fury. The woman remained focused on her phone, talking with Washington, and she'd even asked him to lower his voice, *Allah yuafiquni*. The man, Sinatra, kept his attention on the hotel tower. He said the American William Sloan was inside, an important and valuable man to Abu Dhabi.

That was the only reason Yusuf hadn't arrested them yet —Mr. Sloan.

Yusuf was merely the chief of the special anti-terrorist unit, and already reprimanded for letting a rogue force kidnap Mr. Sloan. The Major General of the Abu Dhabi Police called Yusuf to accost him every few hours for letting this outrage go on, and so did the Minister of the Interior.

If agent Sinatra was correct about Mr. Sloan, his job might be saved.

If Sinatra was wrong, and Yusuf phoned to wake up his superiors this late for nothing, being fired was the least of his concerns.

IN MANNY'S EAR, Bronwen said, "I'm in the lobby. The enormous gorgeous lobby. There are few guests. Everything looks peachy."

The more Manny scrutinized the Conrad Abu Dhabi Ethiad Tower, the more he became convinced William Sloan was inside. The hotel's occupancy looked low. Less than fifty percent, maybe twenty-five. A terrorist group could reserve an entire floor for themselves. With one

Houthi sympathizer on the hotel staff, they could come and go as they pleased, using the garages to hide the abduction. Plus, he had concerns about why the terrorist chose the tallest tower, closest to the ocean.

It was getting harder to ignore Yusuf Torres. The bald special police chief was loud and purple-faced and becoming more so. The chief was flanked by three members of his special forces, reflecting his anger toward Manny—he felt their antagonism like direct sunlight, and he enjoyed it, but they neared a breaking point.

Noelle lowered her cell.

"The CIA finished scanning the Huawei phone you found, Sinatra. They cracked the code, and it's not good news."

Yusuf had been growling at Liya, but his attention was caught. "*Madha?* What phone? What code?"

Liya said she didn't know.

Manny ignored him.

Noelle continued, "According to their Telegram texts, the Houthi have three total targets. William Sloan, an American professor at NYU Abu Dhabi, and a Canadian bank executive working here remotely for the past year. Westerners who should not be in the Middle East, they say. The plan is to extract them to some desert in Saudi Arabia and execute them on a live broadcast, as an example."

"*Ay, vaya.*"

"Who are you talking to?" Yusuf said.

"Our contact in America, who is working closely with Signals, your defense intelligence," said Noelle. "There's more to the Houthi plan than meets the eye, but we aren't sure what yet."

"*Esta es una muy mala noticia.* Bronwen, you copy Noelle?" said Manny.

Bronwen answered through his Bluetooth earpiece. "Yes, I heard. We both did."

Hidden nearby, Junior grunted his agreement.

"Who?" Yusuf pointed at Manny's earpiece. "Who are you talking to?"

"Noelle, did the phone's contents mention Zayn Abdul Aziz?" asked Bronwen.

"Not by name. The terrorists used an Arabic term, *Ansar Qayid*, for great leader, but we don't know who it is."

Manny gazed at the hotel and set his jaw.

"I'm going in."

"*Ya, raqm.* No, American, this is out of your hands now." Sweat poured down the dome of Yusuf's head, and he stood close enough that Manny could smell it.

Manny jabbed a finger at him. "You want to help, Abu Dhabi, you station your men at the garage and stop any truck coming out."

Yusuf's face darkened further.

"Agent Sinatra, I am putting you in my car. Your freedom here is revoked." He spit, pronouncing the final word.

"The devil it is."

"Sinatra," said Noelle.

Manny shouldered past Yusuf. Yusuf shoved, a knee-jerk retaliation. Manny slipped the brunt of the shove, causing Yusuf to lose his balance, and he smacked the bald man. Less painful than a punch, more embarrassing.

Yusuf said, "*Ant sakhif!*"

Too much for Yusuf to endure, he pulled the firearm at his side, a Caracal .40.

Manny guessed it was coming. He slapped Yusuf's wrist with his right hand, grabbed the pistol barrel with his left, twisted inward, and like *that* he was the one holding the pistol. Manny's pulse didn't rise one RPM.

Shock. Disbelief. Yusuf's men went for their own sidearms.

Manny ejected the magazine. Racked the slide to pop the bullet. Pressed the lock and broke the slide away from the grip and let the Caracal fall onto the ground in pieces.

"Don't be petty. We have work," he said.

Yusuf didn't know what to do with his anger, so he sputtered.

"I'm going in. Watch the garage, Abu Dhabi." Again, Manny turned to the hotel.

"*Iietuqiluu hadha alrajulu,*" Yusuf told his squad, and the three men moved to arrest the American agent.

"*Venga, pendejo.*" Manny despised arrogance in men who should have none. He didn't have time to discipline the entirety of Abu Dhabi's police force.

Junior, hidden in the shadows of the parking lot, watched all of this. He spoke into his earpiece, "You want, Sinatra, I can fire a few rounds into the dumbass' car."

Calmly Noelle announced, "My Washington contact is waking up the UAE's Deputy Prime Minister."

Yusuf stiffened and held up his hand.

"*Antazir. Qif.*"

His squad stopped.

"What did you say?"

Noelle read off her phone screen. "Al Shamsi, is that how you say it? The Deputy Prime Minister?"

"*Hafizah allahu.*" The men looked like a ghost had spoken.

"Why? Why would your American call his Highness?" Yusuf looked panicked. He held his hand toward Noelle's phone. "Do not. Do not do this. I will... I can call. Please. Tell them to wait. I will... I will call the Major General first."

Manny was out of patience. He disengaged himself from

the confrontation, no matter how much he wished to smack Yusuf again.

"I'm going in. You stay here and be scared."

"No, no, *raqm*. American." Yusuf swallowed. "I will go too."

"You should not!" Liya broke her silence. "We must be clever and you look like police. Sinatra and I will walk in. We are dressed as a couple."

"No," said Yusuf. "You are not police, not even a man!"

Manny wiped his forehead, angry at Yusuf, at the time difference, at the heat. "*Ay!* They have William Sloan. *My* William Sloan, plus *my* American college professor. I'll walk in and speak with the front desk. Liya goes with me to scare the hell out of them with her government badge, if we need it, and we'll find out what floor they're on. Take your men to the garage door and I'll open it. You follow that, Abu Dhabi?"

He held out his hand. Liya took it, a happy couple.

Yusuf looked near a myocardial infarction.

"Wait." Junior in Manny's ear.

Maldita sea.

"What now?"

"We got a problem," said Junior. "A big one. Look *up.*"

IN THE MIDDLE EAST, the Houthis spread chaos through multiple streams of terror, but none more notorious than their drone strikes—explosive, unmanned machines launched at enemy forces and detonated, utilizing both boats and aerial assets. Their long-range weapon of choice was a small, fixed-winged aircraft powered by a front propellor, like the Samad, capable of flying hundreds of miles. There was no pilot and the only cargo is a bomb.

The Houthis employed a different vessel for short-range attacks. A multi-rotor drone, the kind most readily available to the public, piloted from a nearby controller through a camera. The Houthis used them to maneuver two pounds of plastic C-4 into crowded places like an airport or market.

MANNY LOOKED UPWARD.

As a hive releases a guardian swarm, unmanned aircraft released from the tower. Multi-rotor suicide drones. Piloted by terrorists, probably on the top floor. Carrying an explosive payload.

Manny counted blinking lights. One, two, three... *caramba*, how many did they have.

A cold dread settled in his heart.

"Get back in your cars."

"*Akhris , 'amirki*," Yusuf barked at him.

The murmuration plummeted and the rotors buzzed at a high pitch, like the wings of hornets.

They all looked up.

"*Into your cars!*"

Manny yanked open the rear door of the Maserati. Noelle ducked in, not fast enough, and Manny barreled on top of her, Liya scrambling into the front seat.

The first drone reached the collection of cars and hovered, chest high. A wicked-looking monster with four appendages and angry red lights, moving in twitches. Beneath, gripped in a claw, two pounds of C-4 waited to be triggered.

Yusuf hurled himself over the hood of his cruiser.

The drone beeped. A detonator released a small shock-wave into the C-4. The gases decompressed and a blast erupted at twenty-six thousand feet per second. A mushroom of brilliant light. The car windows shattered. Yusuf's three special forces policemen were incinerated.

Liya screamed.

A second drone snuck under the front bumper of the police cruiser and detonated. The explosion ricocheted off the ground and bloomed upward. The vehicle somersaulted backward, into the Maserati, crunching its roof. The cruiser landed on the far side, wheels ruptured.

ON A BALCONY FAR ABOVE, a man twenty-three years-old removed his virtual reality headset and set it on the dark patio. He blinked to restore his vision, glanced over the railing and smiled at the parking lot and the fire blooming there, almost out of earshot. He crouched beside a waiting drone, clicked it on, and paired it with his headset. The rotors sped up—liftoff. The drone rose to hover over his head and awaited direction. The young pilot shoved his hand into a bag of potato chips, popped them into his mouth, sat back on the chair next to his brethren who also wore VR headsets, and pulled his own back over his eyes. His vision filled with the green night-vision world seen by the drone, initially disorienting. The pilot fumbled for his controller, set it into his lap, and pushed the pitch stick forward.

The drone obeyed, just like playing a video game.

MANNY SQUIRMED through the Maserati's front seats, under the crushed ceiling, and slid behind the wheel. His night-vision was ruined, his ears roaring. He found the key, jammed it in the ignition.

The third drone was blown off course by its sibling's shock wave, tumbling higher before an internal gyroscope found the equilibrium. Now it hunted, red lights blinking, rotating in jerks like an alien. The camera's aperture and night-vision were skewed, the operator flying by a blinded screen.

The drone passed within feet of the Maserati's shattered windshield without seeing them.

Manny started the car, but its engine coughed and died, the battery damaged in the violence. Furious, Manny tried again; the sports car refused to turn over.

"*Out*," he shouted. "Run for the lobby. Beck stay close."

"Oh *cripes*."

Manny shoved his door but it wouldn't open, the metal frame bent. He kicked and the metal squealed.

The drone whirled, a sick mechanical jolt. The camera found the Maserati and locked on. The machine dipped forward like a bull and charged, blades howling. It would detonate in the American's lap. Twenty feet, fifteen—

"Run, my friends!" Yusuf sprang off the hood of his car and fell on the drone. His weight collapsed the aircraft to the ground. The frame broke and the screaming rotors protested. Beneath Yusuf, the payload beeped. He closed his eyes and swallowed. "*Allah yusallmak*."

Manny closed his eyes too.

The C-4 detonated. Yusuf's chest was protected by a ballistic vest; the rest of him disintegrated.

Heat flooded the Maserati's interior. Noxious carbon oxide in their nostrils. The front bumper was thrown. The car spun sideways like a pinwheel, tires scraping and squealing.

Manny's door popped open.

Liya kicked at her own door, once, twice, and it pried loose.

"*Gracias*, Allah." Manny couldn't hear himself say the words. "And Yusuf."

Bright flames were uncoiling from the blacktop.

He helped Noelle slither through the window of her bent door. She smacked at him; his shirt and his hair were on fire. They ran for the hotel.

"*Where* are they coming from?"

"The roof," shouted Manny.

Liya called words that made no sense. She was limping. Manny's earpiece was gone.

More buzzing above.

More insectile drones. Death inbound.

They ran faster.

The hotel's entrance was a work of art in stone, glass, gurgling fountains, flag poles. They ran at the beacon of brilliance, Manny alert, searching, searching...

"*There*," cried Noelle.

Like a spider lowering from its web, a machine fell to block the hotel's entrance.

More predators in the stars, circling, keeping distance from each other's payload.

Drones travel at forty miles per hour; outrunning them wasn't an option.

Manny slid to a stop. The machine at the crest of the stone steps regarded him. Metal and Manny's heart humming.

"You two, back up. Get away from me," he said.

The drone blinked and hovered, amused by the little

dead man. There was no rush. Let him look eternity in the face.

Then, the howl of a super bike. Junior hit fifty miles per hour on his Ducati, tearing through the grass quad and up the short bib of stone steps.

The drone rotated, too late. Junior drove with his left hand and brandished a shotgun with his right, like a knight charging with a lance. He fired at close range, the shotgun blast muted by tinnitus. The machine died in a squeal, fractured into shards. Rotors spun free. The fuselage landed in pieces and the plastic C-4 thumped softly onto the walk.

No eruption.

Junior fishtailed in a slick of rubber, and stopped. He pumped the shotgun to reload.

"C-4 don't blow unless it gets an electric charge. You can even drop that shit and set it on fire. But no electricity, no detonation."

"What?" shouted Noelle. "I'm deaf."

"Y'all look like hell. 'Sept you, Noelle, good as always."

Manny looked to the sky. Three more.

"*Come on.*" Manny grabbed Noelle's hand and pulled. Liya followed.

Bronwen appeared at the hotel lobby's massive entrance. Bewildered, holding a black pistol. "Sounds like Armageddon. I wasn't invited to the party?"

"Suicide UAVs." Junior maneuvered his Ducati through the tall doors into the hotel, sacrilege in the tourist paradise. "It ain't no party."

Ay dios, a small Puerto Rican village could fit inside the lobby. The warm reception, a stylish lounge, modern cuisine restaurant, the wide pool and Arabian sea beyond. A handful of tourists were crying and pouring up the staircases, others huddled at the elevator doors.

Two security guards stared dumbly from the reception desk. Surely they were supposed to do *something*.

Manny grabbed Noelle, grabbed Liya too, and pulled them behind a decorative partition near the restaurant. Panting, bleeding, they peered around the corner. Where was Bronwen?

Three drones remained.

They'd been coming in waves, as though the terrorists had a surplus of drones but only three pilots. The skill the machines were handled with was obvious.

The first drone prowled through the wide doors, filling the entrance with rotor-snarl. Even uglier in the light, black and menacing.

Noelle listened to the dangerous noise but her eyes were fixed on the hidden security guards; they wore stun guns on their belts. She had extensive training in electroshock weapons and knew them to be accurate and powerful. The electric shock would be strong enough to short-circuit the drone, but it might activate the C-4.

The pitch of the buzzing rose and fell, the machine rotating and pushing from the entrance into the lobby.

Junior waited unseen beside the second set of doors and the drone buzzed into range. He squeezed the trigger of his Mossberg twelve gauge. A blast of light and sound ripped at the machine. The drone tumbled, one rotor ruined, the frame pierced but unbroken. It slammed into a post, drunkenly swerved to find its attacker, lost its balance. Fell like a wounded animal.

The detonator coupling held.

A beep.

"Everyone down!" shouted Manny.

The C-4 detonated, cratering the marble floor and blowing apart the reception desk. Impossibly loud. The expanding gases hurled Junior from his bike and through a decorative glass wall which shattered and fell in great wedges.

Bronwen appeared behind a couch and shouted, "*Junior!*" She ran at him across the lobby.

"I'm good! Stay there!"

A loud siren filled the hotel. Fire alarm. Emergency lights flared on the walls.

Through the thicket of smoke, another drone emerged. Quickly the camera latched onto Bronwen. Easy prey. The machine ducked and accelerated, red lights flashing.

Bronwen was exposed and caught.

Manny left the partition. Grabbed a chair from the nearby table. Took two great steps and swung the chair like a club as the drone raced by.

He connected and the machine was smacked sideways. Skittering across the floor, its payload of C-4 was partially dislodged but the claw held. Manny drew his Glock. Both hands, glaring down the sights. Fired once, twice at the beast, *crackcrack.*

Missed both, chips of marble flying.

The rotors revved and the machine lived.

Bronwen wrapped her arms around Manny's waist and pulled him over the partition separating the lounge from the posh restaurant. They fell in a heap, out of sight behind the partition, landing next to the two scared security guards.

The drone regained height, turned, and regarded a lobby without targets.

The third and final machine slowly entered the fray, twitching to look every direction. The two predators took note of the other across the lobby and separated, working in concert. The nearest drone floated directly over Manny and

Bronwen without seeing them, close enough they felt the downwash.

The other slowly worked toward the lounge. Noelle pulled Liya by her hips, backward, backward, slow movements, keeping the partition between them and the roving camera.

Manny grabbed the vest of the nearest security guard. A ballistic Hyperline—thin enough to be concealed but the guards wore them exposed, a visual deterrent.

It might keep Manny's major organs intact.

"Take the vest off," he whispered.

"*Madha qultu?*" The Arabic man was old and frightened.

Manny tugged. "Ay, you're not using it. Take it off."

Somehow, someway, the hotel's phone was ringing at the front desk.

The drones reached the far end of the lobby, near the glass and the pool beyond. They turned and surveyed the scene. Flashing lights, wailing siren, shattered glass. Slowly the machines stalked back, humming and blinking.

There. A target stepped from the restaurant, near the ruined front desk. Not bothering to hide. Manny. The lead drone spotted him. Charged, zero to twenty miles-an-hour in a blink.

Manny raised the pistol. Took a deep breath and aimed. Said, "*Now.*"

The drone zipped past a mirrored support post. From behind it, Bronwen threw a white tablecloth like a net. Perfect aim. The machine flew into the cloth and was shrouded. Rotors sucked the folds in, seizing instantly. Manny fired and fired again, direct hits, momentum carrying the flailing aircraft forward. It landed and beeped and erupted.

Bronwen ducked behind the support post. The mirror burst into a thousand pieces.

Manny covered his face and turned. The shockwave blew him backward, toward a grand hallway leading to the northern tower. The vest protected his torso, the rest burned and hurt like hell.

Pieces of drone radiated outward like shrapnel. Fire bloomed upward and triggered the sprinklers. Water misted the lobby like a spring shower.

Manny rose on his elbows.

"Hay demasiadas de estas malditas máquinas."

The final drone had him. Streaking across the lobby, camera lens as wide as the sun.

He aimed and fired. Closed one eye. Fired again.

Bronwen did too, shooting at the streak and missing, missing, missing.

Manny hit, finally. The fuselage sparked, continued its suicidal flight undeterred.

From her hiding spot next to the partition, Noelle Beck drew a bead with her own Glock.

Like hell she'd miss. That was her partner.

A mystic myopia focused her mind. No fear, no possibility of missing. One shot, leading the monster a millimeter, the pistol kicked. Her bullet connected with the underbelly. Broke the claw. The aircraft veered off course and barrel-rolled. The device beeped. The claw broke. The C-4 payload was catapulted high and far by the tumbling machine. Already triggered, the detonator issued its electric charge and the explosive decompressed.

The eruption caved in part of the ceiling. A myriad of chandeliers disintegrated. The far wall of glass leading to the pool fragmented and collapsed, a tremendous noise.

Debris rained into the restaurant's dining area. Plumbing pipes burst and water gushed onto the tables.

"*Vaya con dios*," Manny muttered.

Bronwen winced at the ringing in her ears. "Is that it?" she called. "Is there more?"

Noelle took a deep breath. "I don't see another." She thought someone should mention her excellent aim.

Liya sat at her feet, hugging her knees.

Sprinkler water misted their faces.

No more buzzing in the destroyed lobby. Only the wail of fire alarms.

The persistent ringing of the front phone finally stopped.

12

———————

They convened at the ruined front desk.

From the stairwell they heard noises of tourists stampeding for the emergency exists, running for their lives.

Junior and Manny were cut up and charred. Noelle's face and her blouse were singed. Liya moved with a limp.

"Where the devil'd they get that many drones?"

"They are common with Houthis," said Liya.

"UAVs are light as hell, easy to transport." Junior was letting Noelle wrap a cloth napkin around his forearm. "Cheap death from cowards."

Manny tilted his face toward the ceiling.

"The pilots are up there somewhere. How'd they know we were coming."

"There are terrorist sympathizers in Abu Dhabi, love. Militant Muslims, betraying their countrymen," said Bronwen.

"Corruption." Liya looked like a woman wishing she'd stayed at her desk. "It is hard to stop."

The hotel's intercom system blared to life. A loud voice boomed, startling them.

"*Ya'teek el 'afye*," said the man. "**Good evening.**"

Across the lobby, in the lounge, television screens flickered to life. At first they displayed a readout of the weather and the hotel's itinerary, inviting guests to attend. But the screens blinked to live feeds from hotel security cameras. Several angles of the lobby, of themselves, of the destruction. Last, a video of a man sitting in a chair. Handsome guy, salt and pepper hair, wearing a stylish suit, shirt unbuttoned at the throat.

He smiled into the camera.

Bronwen made a growling sound. "Zayn Abdul Aziz."

Zaz. The terrorist leader for hire.

"**It is impressive you live.**" His voice came from everywhere. "**It is unexpected. My pilots are good. I congratulate you.**"

Zaz's English was choppy but understandable.

"**I see Bronwen, the *feltene* sent to kill me. I see her Black bodyguard. I see Liya Al Ariani, the Emirates' Houthi expert. And I see two I do not know.**"

"Gonna know me soon, amigo," muttered Manny.

"**I will call the lobby phone again. This time you answer.**" The man held up a cell and dialed, and the lobby phone rang.

No one moved to answer.

On screen, two people were shoved into view. Their hands were bound behind them, their mouths gagged with a dirty rag. Despite the fuzzy image, Manny recognized William Sloan. The handsome man looked angry and tired.

Manny knew the feeling.

"**Answer my call. Or I kill one.**"

"We should answer," said Liya. "Sinatra, you."

"Why not me?" Bronwen demanded. "Zaz and I have history."

"Zayn Abdul Aziz will want a man. It is preferred, especially for extremist Islam."

She scoffed. "Bollocks."

Manny strode to the phone, crunching glass shards. He removed the scorched ballistic vest and he snatched the receiver off the cradle. "You better be calling to apologize."

On screen, the man smiled in surprise.

"*Rayieun.* **Who is this?**" Still he spoke through the intercom.

"A man here for William Sloan."

"**You are a Spaniard.**"

"Even better."

"**Spaniard, I am a businessman. Also I am in a hurry. Make a deal with me. Send up the women and I do not kill William Sloan today.**"

Manny watched the man speak onscreen. His words were delayed half a second.

"How about this deal. Send down the Americans and I do not kill *you* today."

Zaz laughed. The sound echoed.

"**A brave infidel. Brave but stupid.**"

Manny wasn't insulted.

"**It is Liya and Bronwen I want. They cause me pain, so I will take them. And William Sloan lives another day.**"

"William Sloan's gonna live until he's a hundred and ten, *cabrón.*"

"**Tell me. Why does he matter to you, Spaniard?**"

"He's American. And he's my responsibility."

"**Ah. It is your job. Will you die for him?**"

"For America, a thousand times."

"**It is so simple? Duty?**"

"The best things are."

"**He lives if you send me the women.**"

"I'm coming up, Zaz. We talk. And I leave with the two Americans you took."

On screen, Zaz raised a pistol off his lap. Aimed it at the college professor. The picture flared. Over the speaker, a sharp crack. The college professor's head snapped back and he slumped out of view.

The American professor had been executed.

William Sloan closed his eyes and shuddered.

"Oh damn," said Junior.

Noelle put a hand over her mouth. "*No.*"

"I came for them, Spaniard. But I can leave without them. It is five minutes until I leave." Zaz aimed the pistol at William Sloan.

"Don't do it," warned Manny. Sweat trickled into his eyes.

"No!" Liya held up her hands. "*La 'arjuki.* Tell him, no, I will come up! Do not kill another."

"I'll go too." Bronwen's chin was tilted up, a defiant look in her perfect green eyes.

Manny covered the receiver. He couldn't believe them.

"No. Absolutely not."

"You said it yourself, Sinatra. William's your job. We have a duty."

"I don't trade lives."

Bronwen smiled. "Trust me, love. I want to be near Zaz."

"*No.*"

"I get close, I'll kill him. He's *my* job," she said.

"It is your last chance, Spaniard. I leave in four minutes. With William Sloan. Or without him."

"Four minutes. He has a helicopter coming," murmured Noelle. "To the roof."

Bronwen turned on her heel. "Tell Zaz I'm coming up, darling."

"*No!* Bronwen..."

"I'll be back soon, won't I? With William."

It was a lie. Or at least it was blind optimism. Her chances were slim, and the waver in her voice betrayed it.

Liya walked after her. "I will go too."

Manny balled a fist. This was happening too fast.

"*Ay, maldita sea.*"

"I see the women obey orders. That is good. William lives another day, Spaniard."

Outside, ambulances and firetrucks were on approach, sirens growing louder.

Manny threw the phone and it broke against the wall. He pointed at Noelle.

"Beck, stay with Junior. And call Weaver." He ran.

"What about *you?*" she cried.

"I'll be back with William! You stay safe."

The almighty voice. **"Send the women up the elevator. To the penthouse, of course. Only the best. It is not for Allah I do this."**

"Sinatra! Manny!"

He caught the women at the elevator bank.

"Bronwen," he said. "*Alice Worsley*, stop. I'll go, dammit."

The door dinged and opened. She and Liya stepped in.

"I like how you say my name, Sinatra."

"He'll kill you both."

"Maybe not. Zayn Abdul Aziz needs hostages," said Liya. "That is why I go."

"Besides." Bronwen winked. "I'm armed to the teeth."

She pressed a button. The doors slid inward.

"Back soon, love."

"Like hell you will." Manny jumped inside and the doors sealed. The car surged upward with all three.

Liya gaped. "You should not do this."

Bronwen grabbed Manny's arms. "I cannot bear the thought of Zaz killing you. Me, he won't."

Manny snorted. *Zaz kill him.*

"Sinatra. Please. Better me than you."

Over her shoulder he pressed a button. The elevator halted at floor nineteen and the doors opened into an empty hallway.

"This is my stop," he said.

"Thank you, Sinatra."

"You're the best of us."

"I am, aren't I." She smiled. With courage and rebellion in her eyes. "Wait for me."

Manny hugged her. She sensed the trap too late. He picked her up and carried her out of the elevator.

"What! *No!*"

A sacrifice. His life for hers.

She punched and kicked. He tossed her and she stumbled down the hall.

The car dinged and Manny hopped inside again.

"Sinatra, *Manny*, please don't!"

Bronwen found her footing. Turned and darted at the doors.

"Live forever, Bronwen."

Her perfect face, their gazes colliding like fireworks.

She was too far. The doors slid closed, sealing her off.

Gone.

The elevator car accelerated upward.

Silence. Painful silence until Manny took a deep, ragged breath. His heart thundered with relief and fear.

Liya said, "I do not understand. Why did you do that?"

Manny closed his eyes. Thought about what came next.

"Who is she?" asked Liya. "Do you love her?"

"As close as I can."

"What does that mean?"

"If I knew how to love, I already would," he said.

The car slowed and stopped. Manny's reflection in the door parted down the middle.

13

———

A short hallway waited off the elevator. Plush carpet. A marble bust of a falcon. Orchids in a vase on a side table.

After the lobby carnage, this level whispered peace and opulence, distractingly so.

Manny pressed the emergency stop button; Bronwen couldn't use it.

The top floor consisted of four suites. Two armed men waited outside the farthest door, AK-47s leveled at the waist.

"*Arfae yadika. 'aw nutliq alnaari.*"

Liya translated. "Raise your hands or they will kill us and William."

Manny complied.

The men wore khaki pants and faded sports jackets and backpacks. One covered him, the other searched him. His Glock was found and confiscated.

The barrel of an assault rifle was pressed into Manny's back and pushed him forward. He and Liya walked into the large suite. It was a palace compared to most hotel rooms. In the den, men packed electronic equipment. Three of them. Drone pilots.

A dead body lay in the corner. The American college professor.

Zayn Abdul Aziz waited in the kitchen. William Sloan sat at a table, still gagged, eyes wide.

Zaz was more handsome up close.

"No Bronwen." Zaz smiled."It is what I thought."

"I came in her place." Manny saw no one else. Only three pilots, Zaz, and his two armed guards. The moving van team was already gone. "Take me, leave William."

"Do you know what will happen to him?" said Zaz.

"You plan to kill him and show the world."

"It is true. Your information is good. Do you know why?"

"I don't care," said Manny.

"Guess."

"Death to America, Cursed Be the Jews, Victory to Islam, that bullshit."

Zaz laughed. Manny could see why wealthy terrorists trusted him. Zaz was handsome, at ease, charming.

"It is a good guess. But wrong. I do not wish death to America. I have a large house in Miami, on the ocean. The American women..." He grinned at Manny like he understood. Which he did. "Do you know what is good about America? The rest of the world, it fights out of hate. The world, it fights to gain land. To be, ahh, what is the world, selfish. America does not. It fights on behalf of others. Not for itself. It is honorable. Because it can afford to be. It has wealth. But for me? I was born in poverty. Ahh, the word? Scarce. My world was scarce. But now? Never again. I have money and America is a good place to spend it."

"That's why you'll kill William. You were paid. You want more money."

"Yes." Zaz snapped and pointed at him. "It is why. These fools. It is hate. The Sunnis and the Shia and Iraq and Iran and Yemen and... Their hate makes me money. I am generous. It is not all for me. These men too will be rich. And have many virgins in the next life."

"Virgins in hell."

"You believe in hell, Spaniard?"

"God handles things and I hope he'll have me, that's what I believe," said Manny.

Keep him talking, find a way.

"I hope there is no hell." Zaz laughed some more. "For my sake."

"Become a Catholic. Though you might not have enough time for all the Hail Marys you owe."

"It is sad you did not bring Bronwen Davies. I would throw her from a helicopter onto a mosque," said Zaz.

"I was born poor too. But I found a better way."

"Oh yes? What is your better way?"

"Hard work. Sacrifice. America. Something worth living and dying for," said Manny.

"How good for you. I am still looking for it."

"Take me. Leave Liya and William."

Zaz twisted the top off a liquor bottle. Poured himself a drink, brown like bourbon. He sipped and thought about it.

"She almost had me. Bronwen did. It is a year ago now. In Cairo. A close thing. She is very good. To some rich men, I am worth several million Euros. She too was after money."

"Too bad you can't take it with you," said Manny.

"Her Black man is good."

"Junior."

Doors leading to a penthouse balcony were open to the warm night. Air rushed in and their world filled with the sound of a helicopter approaching.

"It is time. *Khudh alfatati. Khudh al'amrikii.*"

One of Zaz's men grabbed Liya by the arm and took her

back through the door, into the front hallway. The other man moved toward William in the kitchen.

With his left hand, Zaz raised his drink. "Spaniard, it is sad, because you amuse me."

Manny had edged near the lamp at the corner of a couch. He said, "*American*. Not Spaniard," and he snatched the lamp, a sudden movement. As he would throw a hatchet, he raised the lamp and pivoted at the waist…

From the kitchen island, Zaz plucked the pistol with his free hand…

Starbursts in Manny's vision, once, twice, three times. Hammer strokes to his chest. Falling backwards onto the carpet. Staring upward at the ceiling, trying to breath.

William Sloan groaned.

The helicopter roared as it lowered to the rooftop helipad, and Zaz closed the door against the noise.

"*Linadhhabi*," he said.

The pilots ran from the room, carrying heavy rucksacks.

Manny's shirt darkened with blood in a line above his belt.

"Americans think they belong everywhere. But you are brave. It was a good thing." He sipped his drink again, and tilted the glass and poured the rest onto Manny's chest and the puckered black bullet holes. "If we reach the same heaven, American, we will drink together. *Mae alsalamati*."

The terrorist left the room, and Manny remained on the carpet. The lamp rolled from his fingers. His eyes closed and a rasp escaped his lips.

The sound of the helicopter faded.

14

____

I'm sorry to wake you, darling. I wish you could sleep longer. But we need to plan.

Manny smiled.

Sleeping was good. Sleeping longer would be *encantador*.

If you don't wake soon, I'll douse you with cold water. I know how much men fear cold water.

Manny didn't fear cold water like other men. In fact he took icy showers.

But not now. He didn't want one now.

He wanted...

Where was he?

Where the devil was Noelle?

He forced his eyes open. He was on a bed, head propped on a pillow, sheets pulled to his waist. The sheets were white and so was the ceiling, and he was thirsty. Everything was too bright.

"There he is." A woman perched beside him.

"Where are we?"

"Room 1010." Bronwen raised a straw to his lips and Manny drank water. "Still in this dreadful hotel."

"Still."

"I couldn't carry you far, could I," she said.

"What time is it?"

"Four in the morning. Local time."

Manny sat up and winced. His stomach was purple and bruised.

Pendejo poured his drink on me.

"That vest you strapped under your shirt saved your life." She pointed at the ballistic Hyperline on the couch, taken from the security guard. "But it was thin, and you'll hurt. One of the bullets broke the skin. Didn't penetrate though."

He smiled groggily.

"I don't die easy."

"I thought you had, when I found you."

"Bronwen. *Mi bonita.* You're never not good-looking."

"I should be angry at you," she said.

"Zaz planned to throw you from his helicopter."

"I'd have taken him with me, wouldn't I."

He smiled more.

"I like you alive and in my bed. Not dead on a mosque tower," he said.

"I called for room service. Hard to imagine, but they stopped cooking due to the terrorists" She indicated the nightstand, covered in snacks. "Fortunately the rooms are shockingly well stocked."

"*Gracias.*"

She unwrapped a granola bar and handed it to him. "Eat. We need to flee."

"Flee."

"Abu Dhabi police think you and I killed the officers in the parking lot and that we bombed the hotel. They already had our pictures from the street fight two days ago, or however bloody long we've been here. We're public enemy number one, not Zaz. With Liya taken and Yusuf dead... It's gone pear-shaped," she said.

"Where is Beck?"

"With Junior, somewhere. They're safe. Quite a couple, those two." She opened another wrapper for herself. "He's upside down about her engagement."

"He should be. She's marrying a criminal."

"Rocky? He reformed. For her. It's romantic." She chewed a bite and watched him. "You fancy her, don't you. Noelle."

Manny felt too weak to be affronted. "Do I."

"It's not love. I know. But it's something."

"It's mostly irritation," he said.

"I'm not jealous. At least not terribly. She's getting married. And I know nothing's happened between you, but still..." She laid down beside Manny and they stared at the same ceiling together. "Still, she has a large piece of your heart."

"So does my coffee maker."

"Don't deny it."

"I'm not. But if I wanted romance or sex..." He finished the granola bar. Balled the wrapper and threw it. "We could have had it by now."

"You'd be good together."

"I doubt it. Not everything that could be good, should be good."

"What if I wasn't around?" said Bronwen.

"I'd find some other British noblewoman. Queen Elizabeth."

"She passed."

"Then one of her daughters," said Manny.

"Princess Anne is seventy-three. Don't you know anything?"

"Why the hell do you have kings and queens, anyway? This is the twenty-first century."

Bronwen laughed and rose. She took her phone from the bedside chair.

"Enough pillow talk, darling. Someone wants to speak with you." She dialed and pressed send.

Manny sighed. He preferred more pillow affairs.

After one ring, Special Agent Weaver answered.

"Good morning, Sinatra."

"It's not good and it's not morning." Manny peered at the window, through the blinds, at the dark world beyond. He'd only been asleep for a few hours.

"Bronwen Davies briefed me about the small war that broke out. I'm in contact with Noelle, who is in police custody and being taken to the American embassy as we speak. How are you?"

"Sore. And angry."

The phone said, "What happened in that hotel suite?"

"I bartered for William Sloan. It didn't work. Zaz shot me and took Liya. His plan is to execute Sloan, and maybe Liya too."

"We thought as much," said Weaver. "Radar tracked the helicopter out to sea. Zaz fled west over the Arabian Gulf, and there we lost him. William's fate would be sealed but for a stroke of luck. Zaz apparently turned back to shore halfway to Qatar and rendezvoused with a convoy near Liwa, far inland. Our military satellites had been monitoring that convoy, driving illegally across the border from Saudi Arabia. Can you believe the new damned Space Force finally did something worthwhile? They unloaded the helicopter and transferred into the trucks an hour ago. Presumably they still have Liya. The convoy is now driving for the border and we can't stop them. We believe they have a camp set up near a recognizable Saudi Arabian landmark, and will execute him there."

"He's being paid well to do it," said Manny.

"Our analysts believe the Iranians are paying Zaz for the abduction, in specific retaliation for the assassination of Qasen Soleimani. It was an incredible blow to the Iranians and the Revolutionary Guard, and they've been searching for covert ways of striking back ever since. Because Sloan is American, his death would anger us and embarrass the UAE and the Saudis too. This would be a huge blow to the geopolitical climate in the MENA region."

"Surely you've alerted the Saudi Arabian government," said Bronwen.

"Yes, but as I said, there's little trust. King Salman is a conservative old man, and his son, the Crown Prince, wants us to butt out of Islamic affairs."

"Saudi Arabia has a king? Embarrassing," said Manny, and Bronwen punched him.

"He's refusing to speak with us, not unless he receives a direct call from the President, which is a definite non-starter. The UAE is more responsive, but they're demanding to know why our agents bombed a hotel and killed their special police chief. Soon, William Sloan will be across the border, and the Emirates will absolutely not violate that line."

Bronwen pursed her lips. "William Sloan is on his own."

"No," said Manny. "He's not."

He sat up with a grunt and threw back the covers.

He was nude.

Bronwen winked. "I had to, for your sake. Or at least, I couldn't stop myself."

"I can't blame you."

Weaver continued, "Sinatra, your team is William Sloan's only hope. He'll be beheaded or burned alive. You must reach him first."

He stood and stretched and his insides complained.

"Tell me how."

"I'm pulling strings at the American embassy. Their hands are tied, but they have back-alley contacts. Unofficially. I think we can commandeer a helicopter and the UAE will turn a blind eye and we'll apologize later," said Weaver.

"Beck can't fly a helicopter."

"Junior can," said Bronwen.

"In these extreme circumstances, partnering with Bronwen and Junior seems advisable," said the phone. "It will never be acknowledged by the government, however."

"Aren't we a plucky team of four." Bronwen yawned and covered it with a fist.

"Rendezvous with Noelle. By then, she'll have more information. Escaping will be tricky, Sinatra. Abu Dhabi's camera system and facial recognition software is everywhere."

"I have a plan." Bronwen stood and threw open the curtains. Outside, the dark ocean stretched into the universe. "We sneak into the water and swim to a nearby, unguarded resort."

Manny didn't want to swim, but it would work. A good plan.

"And besides, darling." Bronwen arched an eyebrow. "You're already dressed for skinny-dipping."

15

They ran unseen through the sand alongside the outdoor restaurant VaKava, which stretched from the Etihad Towers into the water. Behind them, the hotel district was a circus of emergency lights. Ahead, the black sea.

The water was warm as a bath, and just as calm. Manny swam freestyle, each stroke an agony, but the adrenaline flowed and soon his stiff tissues were loose. The current carried them south, away from the lights, a half mile, to the Intercontinental Marina, where they slipped aboard a pleasure cruiser.

The oily water from the marina left them stinking so they showered and raided closets for clothes. In the dark cabins of the bobbing vessel, Bronwen dropped her towel and grabbed him and kissed him and said, "There's never enough time."

Manny balanced between desire and duty, teetering, but America won out. "You told me you want the scenery ever changing."

"If you'd asked me to marry you, Sinatra, in that shopping mall, I would have said yes."

"One day, *señorita*."

An hour after slipping into the surf, they reached the streets of Abu Dhabi dressed in the stylish yachting clothes of billionaires. Bronwen wore a green hijab to cover her blonde hair, and Manny was taken by it.

An SUV braked in front of them, something called a Changan CS75. Junior buzzed the window down. "Get in, you two."

Manny looked longingly at the driver's seat but chose not to press it.

AL BATEEN EXECUTIVE AIRPORT was located in the heart of Abu Dhabi, a landing spot for the world's elite. A place where the wealthy arrived in private jets and the Emirates welcomed them with style.

Junior bypassed the executive terminal, per Noelle's instructions. She directed him toward the service gate, where their contact waited on a small motorcycle. The man flashed his lights, and Junior returned it twice. "That's him," said Noelle. They followed the motorcycle to a barricade, which lowered, and a gate opened and Junior motored into the interior of the small airport.

Manny saw none of this. Both he and Bronwen woke up in the backseat when Junior announced, "We're here."

They stepped out of the Changan and stretched to greet the morning sun. Already the day's heat mounted.

Their contact swung off the bike and removed his helmet. A young guy, maybe twenty-five. Like everyone else in Abu Dhabi, his dark hair and long lashes were perfect.

"Hello," he said in his best English. "Hello. Follow me."

They walked with him around a long hangar to a smaller one, far removed from the terminal.

The empty skies were a watery blue, warming in the east. Runway lights raced down the tarmac on repeat, despite a lack of traffic.

The doors to the helicopter hangar were open and a motorized trolley taxied an Airbus H125 into the morning light. One of the leaner business helicopters. Simple but efficient, used the world over to ferry the rich in groups of four.

"We out of luck, we get into a shootout." Junior'd been hoping for something with bite.

"It'll work." As long as the bar was stocked, thought Manny.

"Here." The young man from the motorcycle led them into the wide hangar. Two other helicopters sat dormant, their blades folded and secured. He searched the hangar until a mechanic whistled to him and pointed to a back table, on which sat two hard-shell shipping containers. "Here. For you, here."

"Thank God for Weaver and her contact at the embassy." Noelle opened the latches. "The embassy said they'd provide a cache of weapons confiscated from traveling Americans over the years." She pushed the lids up. Inside, firmly pressed into foam insulation, was a small arsenal of Abu Dhabi contraband. Two pistols, eight magazines, an M4 carbine, boxes of ammo, tan M-24 binoculars, handcuffs, radios, knives, other gadgets Manny couldn't identify.

His Glock had been confiscated, so he selected an enormous pistol. A Desert Eagle .44 Magnum. Chrome finish. Six inch barrel. Brought to the Middle East by a gun enthusiast showing a lack of discretion. Hard to imagine, but it came in a .50 caliber ten-inch barrel, even larger.

"You Americans and your infatuation with size." Bronwen took the other. "This is preposterous."

Manny nodded his approval, a deep feeling in his patriotic bones. He was himself an eagle. An American bald eagle in the desert.

"Trade you." Junior held out his SIG Sauer, 1911, and Bronwen gladly accepted. Manny took the cuffs, Noelle the radios, and Junior picked up the heavy container with the carbine and walked to the helicopter decoupling from the trolley.

Junior had never flown an Airbus chopper, but in comparison to the fancier machines this would be riding a bike. He loaded his gear and climbed into the cockpit.

He didn't have time to run the helicopter's pre-start checklist. Nor the desire. He clicked on the systems—center console, heating, battery, fuel—engaged the starter and increased airflow through the power turbine. He kept the RPMS low, heating the oil and hydraulics; it would only take a minute because the Middle Eastern sun kept the engine warm. The aircraft came alive and hummed around him. His passengers loaded themselves and latched the doors and more of his panel gave green lights. Fuel boost pump. Anti-collision lights.

He clamped headphones over his ears and tested communication with Noelle.

Voltage and oil pressure and hydraulics were strong. He increased power. At twenty-five percent, the turbine began rotating, driving the transmission and spinning the rotors. He toggled the cyclic with his right hand. Tested the rotor pedals with his feet.

"Welcome to Junior Airways, where a bumpy flight is guaranteed," he spoke over the headset. "Speak now or it's time to rock."

"*Vamos*," came the reply.

Junior said a short prayer.

Almighty God. Hallowed be your name. Your will be done today. Help us save this man, please God, and protect us from evil. Don't let me crash this thing. Amen.

His left hand on the collective, he opened the throttle and pulled upward. The engine whined and rotors increased their speed. The H125 released its grip on the earth and rose. He pressed the left pedal to stop the chopper's rotation. They climbed vertically, twenty feet, thirty, fifty. He eased the collective forward and the aircraft shuddered through ETL. He found the balance between the three controls and packed on speed, the nose dipping. The airport fell away and they were rushing across the city.

Junior hadn't been sure what he would say to aircraft control tower chatter but it never came. The UAE might be officially condemning the American agents, but someone had unofficially cleared the airspace.

The helicopter zipped across the small gulf of water between the city and mainland, and in fifteen minutes they'd left civilization behind, streaking into some of the most hostile terrain on earth.

THE RUB' AL KHALI.

Also known as the dreaded Empty Quarter, part of the greater Arabian Desert that spread across most of southern Saudi Arabia and into the UAE, Yemen, and Oman, thousands of miles of sand dunes and hyper-arid flats. A good place to pump oil or die, often both. Only sparse populations of Bedouins and scorpions survived the never-ending sand, and it was there that William Sloan was scheduled to be executed.

Weaver updated them inflight.

The convoy transporting William had unloaded in Shaybah, a desert town located an hour inside Saudi Arabia, well into the harsh Empty Quarter desert. That area of the world would be uninhabitable except for the super-giant oil field beneath. Oil meant power. Oil meant everything. Through enormous expenditure of human life and money, the Saudis had erected a town there, uninhabitability be damned, and pumped out petroleum.

"There's a dusty airstrip in Shaybah, but you don't have the fuel," said Weaver. "Zaz might shoot you down anyway."

Noelle and Manny were scrutinizing a map of Shaybah. The town was tightly clustered so citizens didn't need to be outside often. During the day it was scorching. Much of their life took place at night.

"Where in Shaybah is he?" said Noelle.

"To the south, technically outside the town, near oasis 'tents' used for gatherings and ceremonies. The town exists entirely to service the oil rigs, and they're paying no attention to the small camp Zaz set up. We believe William and Liya will be executed with Shaybah and oil jacks in the background before the sun goes down today."

"We'll be at the border in an hour," reported Junior.

"Well done," said Weaver. "Set down in Wedhail, a village inside the UAE. A truck will be waiting for you. You'll drive across the border into Saudi Arabia, approaching Shaybah from the north. It'll be a ninety minute drive. Once there, you're on your own. Free William and Liya however you can and return to the UAE, where you'll be under the Emirates' protection. The good leaders of the UAE are growing more outraged by the minute. They're offering to scramble their fleet of F-16s."

"A little late," Manny scoffed.

"Better late than never. In a few minutes, agents, you'll fly out of contact. After that, I can follow you via satellite but your phones will be worthless."

Special Agent Weaver tried forwarding direct satellite feed to their phones so they could get a clear picture of Zaz's makeshift camp but reception wasn't good enough. Soon they lost cell signal and contact with the outside world ceased.

They were alone.

Manny preferred it that way.

16

Wedhail was less a village and more of a sandy outpost between towns on the E90 road. Junior set the H125 down on a strip of pavement behind an abandoned gas station, unleashing a tornado of sand and grit.

He tapped his panel. "It's a hundred and fifteen degrees outside. Damn hot."

"Beck's gonna fry like bacon." As the engine whined down, Manny shoved open the hatch to greet an old flatbed truck rumbling toward them. Heat poured in through the hatch.

An ancient Arabic man kept the engine running but he stepped from the truck and shambled back in the direction of the road without speaking to them. A man who knew his role and did what was asked.

Manny stood beside the chopper and patted the hot fuselage—a good aircraft, a desert eagle in her own right— before climbing into the truck. He wasn't letting Junior drive another vehicle. The rig was a faded green, used to haul machinery, at least twenty years old, made by Mercedes somehow, dual tires in the back, big and heavy. The interior was filthy with rags and grease. Arabic words were painted on the doors, and the glass of the windshield was pitting and cracked with use. More like an old desert donkey. He revved the engine and was pleased to find horsepower.

The cab was stocked with water bottles. Junior carried the hard-shell box and his bag to the cab. He sat on the back bench with Noelle, and Bronwen slid into the co-pilot seat and Manny dropped the truck into gear. Both his heart and the engine began working harder.

"Oh the places we'll go," said Bronwen, staring at the never-ending nothingness.

"One clean shot at Zaz and it's all worth it." Junior opened the case and identified pieces of the carbine. He pressed the bolt carrier into the upper receiver and it snapped home and he asked who the hell thought the gun should be stripped down to its internals.

Manny drove the heavy flatbed twenty minutes and they saw no other vehicles. They'd traveled beyond civilization. Only one official border crossing existed between the UAE and Saudi Arabia—Ghuwaifat, a small town far to the west. Travel there would've lasted four hours each direction. Instead, they would take the unofficial crossing.

Traveling south on E90, a hard-packed dirt road, they reached a sharp turn and stopped. Ahead of them, wasteland. To the left, nothing. To the right, two hundred miles away, Ghuwaifat.

Manny felt the nothingness like hot wind on his face.

Noelle pointed straight. "The borderline is five miles through the desert and then there's a road beyond. A real road, it looks like, used for oil trucks."

He revved the mighty motor. "Then we go through."

They entered the untraveled realm of the Empty Quarter, where William Sloan was being readied for execution. Manny fought against memories of the grisly ISIS killing in 2014.

They didn't dare travel over the dunes' lofty peaks, staying instead to the flats. Their beast of a Mercedes flatbed pulled through the loose sand with ease, all-wheel drive never slipping, motoring through the vast void like a lunar rover on the moon. They rocked and swayed but the winds of time had smoothed out dangerous drops or bumps—there was no danger to the tires.

Noelle had downloaded photos of Shaybah and they scanned them. During the winter, at night, the town could be considered pretty. Clearly effort went into making the place livable for the oil crews. If the town produced liquid power, it was wise to keep the workers happy. But now it wasn't winter and it wasn't night. They poured over the photos and satellite images but planning the assault was impossible. The desert was a never-ending mountain range of sand hills. Weaver explained the camp was set *here*, on a small dune across a flat from the large dune on which the Upper Oasis Tent was set. The two dunes formed a figure 8, encircled by flats and old roads. They could drive around the northern dune, the top part of the 8—which was more than a hill, less than a mountain—or they could go over. Climbing over the northern dune would be slower but give them some surprise.

Weaver's analysts estimated Zaz's manpower was significant. It was more than the team Manny'd seen in the hotel suite. There was no hope they could overpower Zaz and his Houthi militia.

After debate, Manny made the decision.

They would drive to the oasis tents at the top of the large northern dune, and they'd move down the steep decline unseen side toward Zaz's camp, the bottom part of the 8. Noelle would stay with the truck. Manny and Bronwen would scale the southern dune unseen. From long range, Junior would open fire and create chaos, during which the prisoners would be freed. If things fell apart, Noelle and any survivors would drive like hell to safety. If things went well and they got William and Liya out, she would still be prepared to drive like hell to safety, because most likely they would be pursued.

Much depended on how large a force Zaz had. How much firepower. How steep the dune was. If William and Liya could run.

"This won't work. Our plans never work," said Noelle.

"Trust me, baby." Junior ran the action on his M4 and it click-clacked. "Gonna be a terrorist shooting gallery."

They didn't know when they crossed the border, but they spilled onto 95 unexpectedly, a blacktop road nestled in the sand. Noelle pointed and Manny turned east and south, now firmly entrenched in Saudi Arabia. The truck's air conditioning was running wide open but still the heat depressed their spirits. The metal of the truck cooked both above and below, reflected off the road. Harsh sunlight refracted into pieces through the windshield and visibility was low, and Manny was homesick for the smooth roads of America and his own car.

Through the haze, the first oil jacks materialized. The pumps rose and fell above the desert like great hammers, toiling and lonely on both sides of the road. A desolate place that mocked how easy it was to fill a tank at the gas station.

Traffic increased—three trucks lumbered between drill sites. The drivers wore taqiyahs and paid them no attention.

The red range of sand dunes swallowed them, peaks

rising higher and higher, and the road was forced to wind its way through.

Shaybah came into view, dancing in the distance like a mirage.

"Oh damn, that's a real town," said Junior.

From a distance, Shaybah looked like a model kept in a showroom—almost too perfect. Surrounded by an ocean of vermilion sand, the town was well put together and tight, no wasted space, small apartments and commercial buildings within an outer ring of lights and highway.

They drove closer and Manny pointed beyond the town. "Look." Perched at the peak of the dune beyond the tiny town sat a building—the oasis tent, their destination. "We park there."

Noelle handed ear pieces to each member of the rescue team and she paired them.

"It's a radio signal, not cell. I don't know what happens if we move out of sight," she said.

The flatbed circumvented the town of Shaybah without drawing attention. Much of the population was asleep. A ghost town, but complete with stores and restaurants. On the far side, Manny steered up the massive dune, following the winding road, heavy tires pulling through red drifts. The engine roared and they reached the crest in two minutes. They found not tents but small decorative buildings called tents for ceremonial purposes. The world here was too hot for true tents. Manny parked in what little shade he found, away from the ridges that might expose them. He got out and cursed at the heat which hit them like a physical force. The soles of his shoes might melt.

The scent of oil was strong in his nostrils. It pervaded everything here.

They stood at the top of the large dune they'd been

examining on their map. It was larger and broader than they'd been expecting. The planet was nothing but waves of red in all directions, beautiful if not for the sun. They cautiously walked to the far edge of the stones, away from the oasis buildings, to the southern ridge.

There, far below them on a smaller dune, was the terrorist cluster. Manny shaded his binocular lenses so as to not cause a flare, and he examined the encampment.

Six trucks. Eight tents. Two dozen terrorists, seen as silhouettes inside the gauzy shade tents, though rising heat shimmer made counting tricky. Camera equipment. A cage.

A cage.

He passed the binoculars to Noelle.

"They can't stay there long. No human could." Junior was knelt and peering through the scope of the M4 he'd taken.

"They don't plan to. They'll be gone before tomorrow morning," said Manny.

"A cage." Bronwen spoke under her own binoculars, also shaded. "These bastards."

"Can you shoot them from here?" asked Noelle.

Junior shook his head and made minute adjustments on the scope. "A professional sniper might have a chance, but it's too far for me, even with the good Lord's help. The heat gonna mess me up, plus the elevation drop. Gotta get closer."

Bronwen indicated the closest oil jacks. "They'll set the shot with those in the background. Make sure Saudi Arabia is blamed. Let's hurry. I hate to think of Liya in the hands of these Houthi men."

They returned to the flatbed and each drank a bottle of water. They'd be dead in a few hours otherwise. Manny reached into the cab for the Gucci raffia bucket hat he bought for Noelle and set it on her head. She was already too pink.

He finished his bottle and wiped his mouth. "Beck, you think these guys work for Rocky?"

She shot him a *look*. "Rocky owns a shipping company."

"Be easier to call Rocky and ask him to release William, *señorita*, than go down there and die."

"*Hasta tu trasero*," she said and Manny laughed.

"Zaz and Rocky probably go fishing," said Junior.

"Both of you need to *shut up* about my fiancé."

"Zaz is a big fan of America. Says he's got a house in Miami," Manny told them.

"You're teasing." Bronwen wiped her forehead. "Does he?"

"I'm still learning about Islam, but I don't think he's a believer. *Pendejo* was drinking and talking about American women. He's a capitalist, not Muslim. But he's giving us a bad name."

"Can't you be both?" Junior wore a floppy camo Boonie hat. He took it off and poured water into it and set it back onto his head. Pushed his sunglasses farther onto his nose.

"You can't be a capitalist in true Islam," said Noelle.

"Whatever they are in Abu Dhabi, that's the Islam I like. The opposite of Zaz."

"My god I hate that man," said Bronwen.

"Is he worth dying for?" said Manny. "To kill him?"

"The contract is a million. No, I won't die for a million euros."

"You go down this slope with me, it might cost a lot more."

"I'm no longer doing it for him, darling."

"Yeah." Junior hitched the rifle over his shoulder higher. "We decided. Job one is to keep you two dummies alive."

"It's not about cash. It's not about king and country." Bronwen smiled and looked almost sad. "Though for you, I know nothing else comes first."

"For the Constitution, I regret I have but one life. So I gotta do this."

"Where you go, love," said Bronwen, "I go."

LISTENING to the conversation on duty and death, cooking on a sand dune in the Middle East, the far side of the world from her home, Noelle experienced a realization.

She might never love Rocky Rickard.

She adored the man. Looked forward to seeing him. Liked spending time with him. The man lavished her with attention and money. Her engagement ring cost seventy-five thousand dollars; she'd resisted but eventually caved and looked it up. He was handsome. Kind. She could picture herself growing old with him. But would she die for him? Did Bronwen already love Manny more than she loved Rocky?

Where you go, love, I go.

Noelle couldn't say that about Rocky. Not yet. It was complicated.

But love shouldn't be.

Cripes, what was she doing?

"Beck." Manny nudged her. "You with us?"

Noelle blinked. "What?"

"We're going." Manny smiled and said, "You awake?"

Manny's smile.

One thing was for certain. Where Manny went, she went. They were partners. They worked and fought and ate and argued together. Even slept together, in the same room.

The gorgeous blonde hugging his arm, he deserved a woman like her. Fabulous and fit, her blood as noble as that which pumped in Manny, birthright or otherwise. Manny Martinez was the archetype of a man, and Bronwen was his counterpart, and their union was perfect and natural. While Noelle's with Rocky was... what? Convenient?

Was love always an instantaneous bonfire? Could it not build slowly over time?

No woman needed time with Manny.

"*Noelle*," he said.

"Yes." She blinked again. "I'm here. Sorry, it's the heat."

"We're going."

"Manny." She grabbed his linen shirt. "Stay alive. I know you'll die for your country... But please don't."

He winked. "You stay here and stay safe and we'll come back to you." When he spoke, she heard the voice from his mouth and also from the radio in her ear. His voice inside her head.

She and Bronwen made eye contact and they smiled.

Bronwen knew. She knew everything. And she was sweet about it, which was infuriating.

Junior hugged Noelle with the arm not holding an M4 and said, "Sorry for calling you a dummy."

"You stay alive too," she said.

"You a fine-ass Proverbs woman, you know that. Not a dummy."

Then the three of them were gone over the ridge. They skidded down the dune, each step carrying them five feet, the sand cascading, burning grains sifting into their boots, sliding, hopping, to the bottom, demigods descending from Olympus, a four minute trek. Bronwen moved like a gazelle to the left, Manny a cheetah to the right, approaching from opposing sides. A sharp lookout would've seen their dusty descent, leaving trails in the red like animal tracks, but the Houthis were taking shade in the tents, not watching the endless dunes. If death came, they thought, it would be via missile attack from a satellite.

Junior found a rocky outcrop a third of the way down and he knelt on it. In her ear she heard him curse at the scalding heat of the surface.

An ache built in her heart, watching the brave soldiers race toward high odds. What kind of person runs at the violence? Their life ordered in such a way that safety isn't a concern, their convictions set in granite. Their hope anchored in their purpose, faith in the unseen better future. As though already dead, nothing left to fear, playing with house money. The world needed more selfless patriots. While Noelle, the computer analyst, was told to stay back, stay safe. She was no operative but surely she could do more than be the lookout.

She raced back to the hard-shell container and searched through the gear. Another radio. Another set of handcuffs. Two empty pistol magazines. She probed the insulation and felt lumps She lifted the corner of the foam to look beneath.

After college, Noelle had joined the Air Force. No pilot, she worked on systems in the Research Laboratory, including the Directed Energy Directorate at Kirtland Air Force Base. She specialized in non-lethal dazzlers and electrolasers, creating tests to measure the results of plasma channels.

She knew immediately what she was looking at under the foam insulation. A handheld electrolaser, cousin to the PHASR rifle. A big Star Wars looking gun used to deliver high energy electric currents long-range, via plasma channel. She'd used them dozens of times, though their legality was still debated after the 1995 UN Protocol on Blinding Laser Weapons.

She switched on the battery. Green light.

"Are you kidding me," she said. With this, she could make one big explosion.

17

───────

"All clear."

Manny heard Noelle's words in his ears with some static, the whisper of a ghost. He was running up the slope to the Houthi camp and didn't respond.

He knew everything about her, even her breathing patterns, and she'd been lifting something heavy.

The Houthis had arranged six trucks in a barricade between him and the tents, providing good cover for his approach. A Toyota Hilux, three Jeeps, and two old army Humvees.

Their chances were slim. Everything depended on surprise and Junior unleashing hell—make these cowards believe they were ambushed by a superior force, eliminate the nearest threats, leave the rest hiding, and *go,* their retreat covered by an angry man with an M4 carbine.

He put the odds of success at fifty percent.

Forty-five percent.

There was a slight breeze and when it shifted his direction he caught the stench of body odor. Terrorists didn't use deodorant.

The sand muted his approach and he reached the nearest Humvee and crouched next to the tire. Close now to the enemy.

Noelle said, "Manny reached the trucks. He's in position. Cripes, be careful. Bronwen is nearly there on the other side. Still no movement outside the tents. Manny, that truck is empty."

Cautiously he rose and peered over the lip of the window. Keys on the seat. As he'd hoped. Chance of success fifty-five percent. Improvising now, he'd grab William and Liya and get them into this truck. Bronwen too, if he could, otherwise he'd roar down the dune, providing her a diversion. He hated she was down here, exposed, no matter how talented she was.

Quietly, Junior muttered, "Show your face, Zaz."

Manny pictured him cozied up behind his scope, ready to fire.

He crept around the bumper, which burned his hand.

The tents were more like lean-tos, open on one side so the breeze could pass through. Many of the men were asleep. Others reclined and drank from canteens. Two workers inside the tallest, darkest tent were connecting cords from a camera to a computer. The camera was ready on a tripod, aimed at the cage. Inside the cage, William Sloan was lying in a fetal position, exposed to the merciless sun. But alive.

Manny ground his teeth.

There. There was Liya Al Ariani, sitting in her own tent, waiting for death and watching William. She looked tired but beautiful, chin high and defiant. The UAE's terror analyst had been caught by her own subject, and now she'd be slaughtered as an example in the ongoing war between Muslim factions.

She was set apart from the others, inside her own tent, an infidel off limits. Was she tied to the chair? He saw no restraints.

Here was an opportunity. She could be removed from the camp quietly and the Houthis might not notice. Not immediately. Once she was out of danger, Junior could open up. That made one less hostage for Manny to worry about.

He knelt to the hot sand and spoke directly into it to muffle his whispers. "I'm getting Liya out first."

"Roger that," said Junior.

"Manny, Bronwen is there too. She's at the far end of the trucks, closer to the camera."

He tapped the earpiece twice.

He darted from the cover of the truck to the back of Liya's tent and listened. No outcry, no alarm. He crept to the side entrance of the tent and stole inside, moving so silently that not even Liya heard him from mere feet away.

"Manny's inside the tent with Liya."

In the shade, Manny was spared the wrath of the sun. It was ten degrees cooler.

"Liya," he whispered.

She jumped and he set a hand on her shoulder.

"Time to go, Liya."

She twisted to peer at her rescuer.

"Sinatra? *Wall! Ya jeef!* I thought you were dead."

"Shh. See that truck, the big one? Go. Meet me there," whispered Manny.

"You're alive."

"Not for long, we don't move."

She touched his hair. "He shot you, Sinatra. I saw him."

"Can you run?"

"Truly, Americans are powerful enemies. Hard to kill," she said.

In his ear, "Manny's still inside the tent." Noelle's voice was strained.

He said, "Time to go, Liya. Get up."

She stood, favoring one ankle.

"You should not have come, Sinatra. It was foolish."

"That's us Americans, powerful and foolish."

Across the encampment, one of the lounging terrorists stiffened. He sat up and shielded his eyes and peered into Liya's tent. He said, "*Ma hadha?*" He stood and reached for his assault rifle. Couldn't find it, left it in the truck. The two other men sat up too. Followed his gaze. He stepped into the light. He pointed. "*Ya. Ya! 'Amrikiun!*"

Amrikiun.

American.

"They spotted him!" shouted Noelle.

Manny's Desert Eagle pistol roared and a pulpy hole punched clean through the first man's chest. The gun smoked in Manny's fists and he said, "Run, Liya! To the truck. I'm behind you."

Odds of success down to forty-five.

He fired again. The great cannon of a pistol cratering the face of a second terrorist inside the tent, spattering the gauze with gore. *Ay dios*, what a gun.

Shouts around the camp. Men waking, grabbing weapons.

Manny turned to retreat. The element of surprise was lost. Now they were forced—

Liya hadn't moved.

"*Ay, Liya, rapido!*"

Calmly she pressed a little pistol into the soft flesh under his jaw. Her bottomless dark eyes were sad, her mouth mocking.

"Sinatra, I told you it was foolish."

Manny was thunderstruck.

Liya...

She pressed harder.

"Do not do anything stupid, American. You are good but I can squeeze so easy."

"Wait!" In Manny's ear, Noelle shouted, "WAIT! Bronwen, Junior, *stop*. They caught him! Liya betrayed us. Bronwen get back. Regroup. If you charge now, Manny's dead."

"Ah damn it, I never liked that little girl. *Shit*," said Junior.

Liya watched him carefully.

"Drop your gun or I squeeze, Sinatra."

"Everyone in the Middle East," said Manny bitterly, "is a terrorist."

Houthi men ran from their tents holding rifles and pistols. They saw Liya with her gun in Manny's throat and they stopped cold.

"You understand, American, these men do not see it that way. They are freedom fighters. They fight for Allah. For Zaidi and Yemen. You are the terrorist," she said. "Drop your gun."

He did.

In his ear, "Help me, guys. What do we do now?"

"Damn. There's our boy Zaz, *right there*. I take the shot, Bronwen?" said Junior.

"*No*. They'll kill Sinatra. We'll find a better way."

Liya tilted her head. Reached to Manny's ear and plucked out the earpiece. The voice of his allies silenced.

"*Awh la*," she said.

"I haven't read the Quran, Liya. But I read the Bible. Something about justice for the innocent."

"No American is innocent. They are corrupt, oppressive enemies of Allah."

"What about love your enemy? Read that part? Pray for your enemy, turn the other cheek, all that," said Manny.

"Is that why you are here, Sinatra? That man you killed seconds ago, why did you not pray for him?" She raised the earpiece for all to see. She spoke in Arabic, "*We must hurry. This man did not come alone. There are others.*"

Manny's pistol was pilfered from the sand. His arms forced behind him. His head swam with memories from the previous days. Conversations about the unknown traitor in Abu Dhabi.

On the flight over, Weaver told them, *The CIA believes the Houthi movement has sympathizers inside Abu Dhabi.*

Manny shouted at Yusuf over breakfast, *There's a Houthi traitor in your force, Yusuf. Our government called you, and the traitor sped up William Sloan's abduction.*

Bronwyn recently reminded him, *There are terrorist sympathizers in Abu Dhabi, love. Militant Muslims, betraying their countrymen.*

At their stakeout, Liya had climbed into his car and seduced him for information, for his sources.

In hindsight, it was crystal.

Liya was the traitor, the Houthi sympathizer.

Zayn Abdul Aziz stepped into Liya's tent. He wiped his forehead and the back of his neck with a handkerchief. He wore a linen shirt dappled with sweat.

"American! You look far better than when I saw you dead on my floor. It is good you came."

Liya held up her hand. She spoke to Zaz in Arabic and he fell silent.

Caramba. Liya was the brains? The boss?

But in her patriarchal world, she needed a man to lead. To be the voice and face. Manny's head swam.

She lowered her gun from Manny's chin. She stepped to Zaz and they embraced and kissed, briefly, and Manny got the impression of serpents intertwining. She handed Zaz the earpiece.

"He is not alone."

"You betrayed your people, Liya." Manny's arms were painfully wrenched backward.

"My people? I had to explain the difference in Muslims two days ago. What do you know about my people? Could you find Yemen on a map? You know nothing." She reached into Manny's pocket and withdrew the handcuffs she saw there. "What I know is this. Death to America. Victory for Islam."

Manny shot Zaz a questioning glance. "Death to America? What about Miami?"

The man shrugged. "She has more hate than I do, American. It is she who hired me, for the Houthi cause."

"Tie him to the trucks," she said.

Zaz addressed the crowd of men in Arabic. "*My brothers.. This man has allies. Be careful. We will make this American the example, now, and we leave camp in ten minutes, if Allah wills. Hurry, brothers, put him in the cage and attach him to the trucks.*"

A Houthi gunman raised his rifle and smacked the back of Manny's head, and Manny's knees gave out.

His chances of success, like the world around, were dim.

...tie him to the trucks?...

18

Noelle Beck was watching a nightmare. A nightmare through binoculars.

"That bitch," she seethed. "That *bitch*."

"I can't see over the tents. Talk to us, baby. What's happening," Junior said, through the earpiece.

"Manny is handcuffed. He's on the ground, not moving. Liya is opening the cage. Oh *cripes*." Noelle pulled her gaze away and scanned the line of trucks. "Bronwen, where'd you go?"

"I'm in the jeep, darling. And guess what I found. Suicide vests. Grenades, these cheeky bastards. I'm going to make a fuss when it's time," she whispered. "Hope isn't lost yet." She slithered out of the jeep and ducked by the gas tank.

"They're removing William Sloan from the cage," said Noelle. Her stomach knotted until she might vomit. "The men, they're... Some men are packing. Be careful, Bronwen. They'll be loading the trucks soon."

"I dearly hope so," she said, her voice distorted with static.

"I think they're filming?" Noelle's pulse raced. "Zaz is wearing a mask and he's talking to the camera."

"Oh I got him. I got Zaz now. Wanna pull this trigger so bad." Junior's position was close enough now he wouldn't miss.

"Not yet," whispered Bronwen.

"They put Manny in the cage. *They put Manny in the cage!* He's... What're they doing? They're attaching him to chains. Chains on his wrists. Another around his waist. I can't... I can't see." Noelle stood and ran to a different spot to get a different view. "I can't see what they're doing! Manny, wake *up*!"

"I can see." Bronwen's voice finally carried a trace of panic. "He's in the cage, attached to two trucks. They're going to pull him apart."

Noelle's mind couldn't force that to make sense. Those words didn't go together.

"They're *what*?" she asked.

"Two trucks driving in opposite directions. He's chained to both. We've got to *move*."

"I'm ready to fire, baby. You can't take my boy without a fight," said Junior.

"Okay, okay, oh cripes, our plans never work." She had moved a heavy clay planter from inside the oasis tent to the lip of the dune, and now she hefted the bulky electrolaser gun. She lowered it onto the planter and ducked behind it. Pressed her shoulder into the stock. Clicked on the battery and activated the laser sight, and she peered through the scope.

"Junior. I need gasoline," she said.

"What?"

"I can't punch through metal. But I have electricity. I can make fire."

"Girl you're talking crazy shit," said Junior.

"Just *trust me*! Give me gasoline, but not near Bronwen, and *hurry your ass up*!"

Manny's head screamed.

He was in the sun, baking, the back of his skull bleeding. The world a fuzzy agony. He tried reaching for his head but a chain prevented the motion.

It seemed another life when he was splashing through the Arabian Gulf mangroves. Water. That would be nice. Water everywhere.

He sat up, ignoring the protests of his aching abdomen, aching brain. He spit out sand.

His hands were cuffed before him, attached to a chain that ran between the bars of his cage. The chain got lost in the sand but he saw the eventual end attached to the hitch of the Humvee. Another thick chain was looped twice around his middle like a belt, snaking through the opposite side of the cage, to the Toyota.

Ay dios, they were going to rip William Sloan into pieces.

Now, that's what would happen to *him*.

He pulled at the cuffs but they were too tight.

The cage was constructed of welded rebar. Not tall enough for him to stand. There was no floor, only burning pebbles. He could push the cage up and over, *maybe*, but he was attached to chains that ran through the bars. It'd do him no good.

It was *so* hot. The rocks scalded his butt through his pants. More pressing than the heat, fear built in his chest.

Focus, Manuel.

Zaz was making a speech in Arabic for the camera. A

call to resist, to serve Allah? Was he implicating Saudi Arabia? Tents were dropping, men packing camp. The rest stood somber for the execution. Liya watched from her tent, next to William Sloan, who lay prone at her feet.

The Houthis knew Manny's friends waited nearby. They were killing him and hauling ass.

He wiped his forehead and the chain clinked and beads of sweat dropped onto the handcuffs.

LIYA FELT HATRED LIKE A HUNGER. She'd worked for months to hire Zayn Abdul Aziz, resorting to sleeping with him to lower his fee. She spent weeks selecting targets, arranging the abductions, only to have the Americans show up unwanted, unwelcome, as they always did. This handsome one in the cage chased them across the water, through the streets, refused to go home when ordered, somehow arrived at the university, surprised Zayn Abdul Aziz in the hotel tower, destroyed her drones, survived being shot, and tracked them into the barren deserts of Saudi Arabia. It was impossible!

She hated him most of all.

In seconds his body would be broken. Arms ripped from their sockets. His torso squeezed in half. She assumed. She'd never seen it done. In the past executions had been simpler but she wanted to escalate their cause, working on behalf of the ah-Houthi family.

On behalf of Ansar Allah.

She kicked the man on the sand, William Sloan. His time would come soon.

If Zayn would hurry! This was taking too long!

She knew the American wasn't alone.

MANNY WORKED THE HANDCUFFS, scraping them against his wrist until the skin bled. No use! Too tight. These weren't cheap cuffs, but a nice set made in America...

He twisted his wrists to examine them.

These were *his* handcuffs! The set he'd taken from the box. She cuffed him with his own restraints.

Hope flickered.

"No entrance exam to be a terrorist," he mumbled.

Zaz's voice rose in pitch. He was brandishing a long black knife as a prop, pointing at the sky and at the American. He achieved a feverish pitch, earning his money. Men climbed into the Toyota and the Humvee and started their powerful engines. The Humvee inched forward and the slack in the chain attached to Manny's wrists was disappearing like a viper writhing in the red sand. In a manner of seconds he would be pulled apart at the joints.

Awkwardly he rose to his knees. Out of time.

LIYA SHOUTED at the men to hurry. Some of them listened and some didn't. Few had known about her before yesterday, and there'd been a minor revolt when her leadership was discovered. A woman leading? Impossible. Her control over them was tenuous and she'd screamed at them that no one would be paid if they didn't obey.

She watched the trucks drive in opposite directions, sucking up the chain slack, willing the drivers to stomp the gas...

JUNIOR FIRED, *about damn time*. The M4 bucked smoothly, and the big 5.56mm slug tore a hole through the jeep's fiberglass panel near the gas tank. He shot again, another puncture wound, and this time he saw gasoline leaking, a drizzle of reflected sunlight disappearing into the desert floor

"There's your gasoline! The middle jeep!"

He swung his scope upward.

To the masked face of Zayn Abdul Aziz, the man worth a million dollars. Steadied...

Far above him, at the crest of the dune, sweltering, sweat in her eyes, Noelle didn't reply. She was holding her breath and centering the red dot on the ruined gas tank. The scope wasn't powerful enough and this would test the range of the electrolaser rifle.

Keeping the red dot steady was impossible!

She pressed the trigger.

A powerful laser shot out, invisibly connecting her gun to the jeep, forming a conductive plasma channel. A millisecond later, quicker than thought, the gun released its charge, a powerful electric current. She essentially *tased* the jeep and its leaking gas tank, flooding it with electricity. The metal superheated and sparked and the gasoline caught in an instant.

In her periphery, Bronwen threw a grenade, hell unleashed...

∽

ZAYN ABDUL AZIZ screamed and stepped aside, so the camera had a full view.

Liya's heart fluttered. She felt the American's blood in her mouth.

At Zayn's scream, the drivers gunned their engines, flinging sand.

At that moment, several discordant things happened she did not understand.

Gunshots rang out. From her own brothers?

The face of Zayn Abdul Aziz disappeared, as though struck from the side by a giant hammer. One second he stood exultant and powerful, the next his mask was punctured and torn, his eyes vacated, his body staggering, stumbling, and one of their vehicles blew like a bomb.

"*Raqm*," she breathed.

A tremendous blast that hurt her ears and a jeep came off its wheels, fire melting sand beneath. Screams. A second later, another truck blew, a great lotus of debris rising. Missiles? Fighter jets?

"*Raqmu! 'iinahum al'amrikiuwna!*"

No, no, NO NO, they were too late, all of it falling apart!

More gunfire. The body of Zayn Abdul Aziz falling before the camera. Trucks roaring, chains tightening, at least the American would die messily on camera...

Blooming fireballs and Zaz gagging on blood outside the cage.

Manny awkwardly snatched the handcuffs key from his pocket—they hadn't bothered to search him.

Pinching the key between his slick fingertips, he slammed it home, twisted, released one hand, dropped the key into the sand, scrabbled for it, slid it into the second keyhole, twisted, *free*, metal cuffs falling into red rocks. He survived by a half second; the Humvee's chain snapped the handcuffs out of the cage at twenty-five miles per hour.

Manny gulped, relieved his hands weren't attached. He twisted inside the heavier chain he wore like a belt. Got the loop over his head, shoved himself *free* as the chain tightened and slammed into the bars. Manny ducked and covered his head. The force of the Toyota truck bent the rebar and ripped the cage off the desert floor, like pulling a Band-aid, the metal missing Manny by inches.

Men shouting, diving to the ground, firing assault rifles uselessly at surrounding dunes, at the attackers everywhere.

Liya.

Red-faced, hate making her ugly. She raised her pistol at Manny, who stood unarmed ten feet away.

"'*Akrahuki. Mut!*"

That was no compliment.

A miracle then—William Sloan, laying at her feet, kicked her. He put the toe of his boot hard into her knee and she yelped and fired wildly and staggered into the gauzy tent wall. As she tried to right herself, Manny crossed the distance and took her gun away and shoved her into the hot sunlight.

"Lay down with Zaz and die for Allah," he said.

"'*Akrahuki. Mut! Akrahuki*" she screamed again. Weaponless she ran at him, clawing, and he shoved her harder and she fell.

Across the camp men spotted him, aimed assault rifles, shouting words he didn't know, and Bronwen strode into view behind them, angel of death. She plucked an assault rifle from a fallen tent and she cut them down, the deadly chatter of an AK-47, and they turned too late, already dying. She emptied the clip into the fallen bodies—overkill. Better safe than sorry.

She dropped the empty rifle. Stepped over shattered flesh and handed Manny his Desert Eagle .44.

"You're a lot of trouble, love," she said.

"I'm worth it." He helped William Sloan to his feet. "*Amigo*, you're not as helpless as you pretend."

William grinned, his face burned, lips chapped. "No, but water would be nice."

"An entire ocean of it." He held out his hand to Bronwen. "Let's go, *señorita*. I'll drive the Humvee."

"I have a better idea, love, and you're not driving." She tapped her earpiece. "She's here, that darling girl of ours."

FOR A HORRIBLE MOMENT, Noelle thought the big flatbed truck would somersault. She drove it full speed over the lip of the dune, the horizon vanishing upward, the nose plummeting, plummeting, her stomach in her throat, falling downward until the front bumper plowed into a drift on the downslope, rear wheels crashing, her windshield nothing but red, a plume of sand erupting, Noelle thrown into the seatbelt, the tires churning, engine bravely roaring, the vehicle emerging like a submarine surfacing through a crimson wave, down again, wildly down, bottoming out on the flat, Junior up and running beside her, reloading as he did, shifting gears, Noelle screaming like a crazed warrior, up the far dune into the Houthi encampment. Over a dozen terrorists still lived. They fired at her, heavy thumps into the blessed metal doors of the truck, and she drove *through* the remaining jeep, pushing it ahead of her like a plow, into the tents, crumbling the camera, and finally braking, grinding the lifeless body of Zaz into the sand.

"GET IN!"

Doors banged open, gunfire crackling, Junior dropping terrorists, six kills so far, and Manny shoved his rescued hostage into the back. Bronwen climbing into the passenger seat, Junior shouting, "Go, go, step on that gas, baby!"

Noelle stomped. The truck lumbered forward, Junior leaping onto the wide bed and flattening to avoid incoming rounds.

"Ay, beautiful driving, Beck!" Manny laughed and ruffled her hair from behind.

"Get your hands off me! We're not out of this yet!"

The Houthis fired at the big flatbed that retreated down their dune and out of range.

LIYA SCREAMED to get the attention of her depleted insurgents. Screamed so they wouldn't waste their ammunition.

Into the trucks, she told them. They still possessed two functional Humvees and a Toyota.

This wasn't over. She'd die first.

Noelle's right foot never left the floor, keeping the truck's gas pedal mashed. They trundled back onto a real road and gained speed. The vehicle leaked red sand like a dragon did fire inflight.

They roared around the town of Shaybah, still sleepy and ignorant of the small war. Noelle passed oil jack trucks in the wrong lane, warning them with her loud horn. At the first oil refinery station, she pulled sharply onto Highway 95 —a highway in name only for it was vacant.

William drank down a half bottle of water and spoke in a gravel voice. "I don't know if I'm worth this."

"America and freedom and democracy, *señor*. That's who are you."

"I wish I'd left with you immediately, at the Shangri-La," he said.

"And miss all this fun?" Bronwen grinned at him and William was struck speechless by it. "Better to die a hero than die old, Mr. Sloan."

"This as fast as she goes?" Manny spoke loud over the engine.

"It's floored," replied Noelle.

He peered at the speedometer. "110?"

"That's in kilometers. We're going..." Noelle did quick math. "About seventy."

"They'll catch us." He turned on the rear bench and slid the glass window hatch open. Junior leaned against the cabin's rear wall, gun across his lap, keeping watch. "How's your ammunition?"

"Low. And here they come."

Far back, shimmering and dancing like apparitions, Liya's three trucks gained ground. Her Humvees traveled closer to eighty than the Mercedes flatbed could.

Manny slid through the back window awkwardly and stood on the bed, braced against the cabin's roof. Furnace wind tore at him.

Junior tilted his head back. His floppy hat was secured under his chin.

"Gonna need so much aloe."

"I don't feel the burns anymore," Manny shouted. "That's a bad sign."

Bronwen's face at the window. Big green eyes. "Twenty miles to the border. We need to hold out that long, says Noelle."

Junior patted his rifle. "Only got the one mag left."

"Like Jesus with bread and two chickens feeding the people, it'll be enough."

"It's fish, you heretic." Junior laughed under his reflective sunglasses. "Chickens my ass.'

"Ay, whatever, don't miss." Manny squatted at the rear window, nose to nose with Bronwen. "Stay in there."

"Why?"

"I'm your boss, that's why."

"My boss, what a hilarious thought," she said. "Would be hot, though, wouldn't it."

"America is the boss of England, everyone knows that. Stay in there, keep your head down."

"I'm getting the Noelle-treatment now? You must really fancy me." She reached through the window, took his face, and she pulled him close and they kissed. "I'd do it all again, love. This ride of ours."

A pang of fear in his chest, looking at her. Each meeting the others gaze like it could be the last.

"Look!" cried Noelle.

On the rim of the world, against a fading blue sky, two fighter jets cut across their horizon. As they watched, the jets cut a perfect arc and raced back the way they came. Their contrails made overlapping U-shapes. Too far to make out details, the jets existed as indistinct guardian angels.

"They're patrolling the border." Manny watched the silhouettes with a hunger, a new appreciation for air superiority.

"F-16 Falcons." William Sloan drank more water to lubricate his voice. "From Al Dhafra Air Base, outside Abu Dhabi. The United Emirates invested heavily in them."

Falcons. Manny wished they were Eagles, but the Falcons were made by Lockheed Martin, an American manufacturer, so it would have to do. He nodded to himself.

"They won't cross the border," said William. "Saudi airspace is sovereign."

"But once we do..." Twenty miles. Those F-16s had launched after a phone call from America? From Weaver? Manny smacked the roof of the truck. "Make this thing move faster!"

"I'm trying!"

Bronwen pointed beyond Manny, to the road behind. "The Houthis, love, they're here."

The red Toyota Hilux had left behind the slower Humvees and closed on the flatbed at ninety miles per hour, materializing out of the gleaming heat and dragging a chain from the hitch.

"Get in here," said Bronwen. "With me."

"They can't hit us. We're a moving target." Manny asked for his Desert Eagle and she handed it to him. One problem with the gun, it was too big to wear, not without a special holster.

A twinkle of gunfire from the Toyota.

A bullet whined and caromed off the flatbed. Another blew off Noelle's side mirror.

"Can't hit you?" said Bronwen.

Manny lay prone on the flatbed to be safe and he drew a bead on the Toyota. Too far to realistically hit. Five bullets remained in his gun, though he thought Bronwen had more. He removed the compact M-24 binoculars folded inside his back pocket, and peered at their pursuers.

Junior lay beside Manny and spoke over the slipstream.

"Wish this M4 had a bipod."

"You killed Zaz. You can afford one," said Manny.

"Maybe. Been thinking about getting a retainer with the money. One of those invisible ones to fix a smile, you know?"

"You have a great smile, *amigo*."

"I do. God is good. But I ain't happy with the canines," said Junior. "Could be straighter."

Manny lowered the binoculars. "Show me."

Junior smiled big at him, teeth bit together, bouncing on the flatbed.

"Beautiful. Nothing to worry about there."

"You think?" said Junior.

More twinkling gunfire from the Toyota, snapping at the air but missing the truck.

Manny glanced at his watch. Fifteen, sixteen miles to go.

Junior peered into his scope at the truck, a hundred yards back. "Oh damn, they got rockets."

One of the Houthis hung out of the passenger window. Holding something big on his shoulder. A rocket launcher. Alarm raised Manny's hackles.

A pop of light and smoke. The rocket released and the Toyota swerved.

The inbound was a PG-7VL—anti-tank, highly explosive. Unguided, cheap and deadly. Fired clumsily from the racing Toyota, the rocket touched down halfway to the flatbed, skidded off the road at six-hundred miles per hour, touched again and detonated forty feet from the rear bumper. A thunderous boom and flare of fire, brighter than the sun. Fragments of the blacktop blew as from a volcano. The shockwave hammered their eardrums and tossed the flatbed's rear bumper to the side, tires squealing. One of the four rear tires shredded, coming apart in thick rubber strips that flayed the undercarriage.

The Toyota slowed and veered around the crater, off road.

"RPG-7s," shouted Manny.

"Can't aim though."

"They're reloading."

"No shit," said Junior. "Cheap-ass rockets piss me off." He braced an elbow on the flatbed and held the stock of the gun steady. "Too far for this."

"Do it anyway."

"I am."

The Toyota closed. The Houthi slid out from the

passenger window again. The shoulder launcher was awkward and threatened to tear out of his grip. The rocket's exhaust would counter-balance the propulsion, so the user wouldn't be thrown.

At a cost of only a few thousand, every terrorist owned an RPG-7. Easy to use, reloading in seconds.

The rocket launcher aimed at them, the Houthi fighting the wind and his swerving Toyota. Steadied.

Junior took a breath, released half, held it, and placed his finger on the trigger.

Two cracks from his M4.

The Toyota's windshield punctured twice, reflecting a thousand skies. The truck turned sharply as though side-swiped, cut off the road, went up on two wheels, pitching the rocketeer out of the window. A howl of rubber. The launcher fired directly downward, unloading the explosives into the desert floor. The explosion bloomed upward and threw the Toyota. The vehicle spun airborne in a tight smoking barrel-roll, shedding parts, and landed out of sight in the red rocks.

"May God have mercy on their souls," said Junior.

"They're about to learn some unexpected truths about Allah. Like he doesn't hand out virgins to terrorists who can't aim."

"Got that right, brother."

They were cut short by another rocket. Fired from a thousand yards, issued by the lead Humvee. The rocket streaked over their heads and detonated against a dune beside the road, a fountain of dust into the evening blue.

For the first time, the sound of the powerful F-16s reached them, the General Dynamics engine a welcome distraction.

Ten miles, thought Manny? Nine?

"There's Liya," said Junior, behind his scope.

Manny raised his binoculars.

Liya was visible from the waist up, standing through the Humvee's opening in the roof. Her hair streamed behind, a wild demigod. If she killed her prey, she might still work in Abu Dhabi unsuspected, the lucky survivor of a terrorist plot.

"Woman's passionate." Manny twisted to look at the F-16s. Maybe the pilots had seen the rocket detonations, maybe not. "Be good if this truck had flares."

Junior shouted over his shoulder. "*Bron!* Get the flares from my bag. Light'em up. We need to communicate with the Falcons. Let'em know we're here."

Another rocket roared by, close enough they heard it hissing, cratering the ground to their right, sand hurled into the sky like a viper uncoiling.

Inside the cab, Bronwen rifled through the backpack Junior never traveled without. She found a pack of four and handed one to William. They each ignited, bright fire in the cabin and the odor of sulfur. They thrust them through the windows and held tight.

Look at us, F-16 Falcons! We're over here and we're friendly.

On the flatbed, Junior said, "Bet the Humvees' glass is bullet proof."

The Humvees neared, able to move ten miles per hour faster than the Mercedes truck. The thousand-foot gap narrowed to seven hundred, to three hundred, and soon their rockets wouldn't miss, now only a handful of miles from the border.

A man stood from the first Humvee. He shouldered his RPG-7, took aim, and fired quickly. The rocket moved faster than sight but the world shattered directly to the right of the flatbed. Impossibly loud. The road caved in as the flatbed rolled over it, wheels thrown sideways. Another of the quad tires popped and shredded. Manny and Junior gripped handles in the flat surface to keep from sliding off.

"Bullet proof or not," shouted Manny and his Desert Eagle spoke. The heavy .44 round ricocheted off the Humvee's windshield and the rocketeer ducked back inside. He fired again, a direct hit. Junior fired his M4 but the windshield held.

In the second Humvee, farther back, Liya lowered into the safety of the impenetrable fortress.

Getting desperate.

The Humvees enormous now.

"We're going off road!" shouted Noelle. The blacktop ended and they raced into the sand, immediately bucking and losing speed. Two miles separated them from the border.

"The tires," shouted Manny, knowing their bullets wouldn't puncture the thick military-grade rubber. Nothing left to do but try.

He fired twice at the front tire, not sure if he hit. Junior did too, from fifty feet. No effect.

Still the flares burned. The F-16s were close enough that their armament was visible. Four deadly air-to-ground SLAM-ERs.

One bullet left in Manny's Desert Eagle.

Close enough that Manny could see the face of the Humvee's driver. The clumsiest terrorist in the Middle East wouldn't miss at this range.

The Houthi rocketeer again, hauling up the long RPG-7. Placing it onto his shoulder and catching his balance.

Death for the flatbed.

"Take him down," shouted Manny.

Junior glared through the erratic scope, fired and

missed. Fired and missed again, the spark of a ricochet off the roof.

One bullet left, Manny tracked the man with the sights of his pistol. Locked him firm between the front and rear...

Manny fired.

The Houthi took the .44 round in his stomach and he depressed his trigger.

Launch. Smoke.

The rocket impacted the road beneath the Mercedes. Designed to ruin tanks, the truck was a far easier victim. Detonation, tires melting, the depleted gas tank igniting, axles destroyed. The flatbed was tossed upward and the cabin tilted forward onto its front wheels. Manny and Junior were catapulted into the air, their clothes on fire.

20

———

The two UAE Block 60 F-16s had taken note of the incoming gun battle, watching insulated from five hundred feet in the air. Each fighter was canted at forty-five degrees to provide the pilots an angle to see the Saudi desert. Neither carried a belly-camera or operator; ground surveillance wasn't their normal mission.

Beneath them, south of Jereirah, a convoy of Abu Dhabi military jeeps barreled toward the border, a rescue operation too far to help. The pilots ignored these and kept their gaze glued to the miniature trucks and their desperate race out of Saudi Arabia.

When the lead vehicle lit flares, the pilots radioed it in. The air traffic controller, referred to as *Burj Sufrin*, the Sovereign Tower, responded to standby.

The F-16s continued their surveillance. Orders were orders, and they were not to engage beyond the sanctity of the UAE, not unless fired upon, which was an alarming possibility. Houthi terrorists were known to have cheap SAMs.

While they waited, a Signals officer spoke over the

phone to an American monitoring a military satellite—an American watching with her team, who'd seen the flares, who hadn't taken her eyes off the flatbed for thirty minutes. They spoke. The Signals officer relayed the strong request to the liaison of the Executive Council, and received a quick reply from the enraged Deputy Supreme Commander of the Armed Forces of the Federation.

The F-16s were issued new orders.

Sovereign Tower — Gazelle Six, you are cleared to enter Saudi airspace. Engage southern two targets. Do not fire on northern truck. Repeat, do not engage truck designated by flares. You are authorized for guns only. Repeat guns only, engage and destroy southern two targets.

Gazelle Six — Copy that tower, engaging southern two targets with guns only.

The lead Block 60 F-16 peeled away from the flight path and dropped altitude. He descended to three hundred feet. On his forward screen, the two Humvees abandoned the highway to pursue the flatbed through the fringes of the Empty Quarter. He didn't know who these people were and he'd never be told.

He centered the lead Humvee in his digital crosshairs and steadied his aircraft. He closed to guarantee accuracy, and toggled the trigger. The six-barrel Vulcan 20mm cannon erupted beside the cockpit. He fired for two seconds, releasing two hundred rounds.

On his screen, the lead Humvee fired a small RPG at the laboring flatbed truck, and then his rounds landed. A strip of destruction tore the sand and walked into the lead vehicle, which crunched inward and shattered into pieces, no match for the M50 ammunition. The fuel tank blew, a bright fireball. The final bullets sheared off the front driver-side wheel of the second Humvee and it rammed into the first at sixty miles-per-hour and vaulted airborne. Bumper over bumper, the second vehicle somersaulted.

The devastation was remote and silent.

The pilot pulled his fighter jet away, too close to the ground, for another strafing run.

Gazelle Six — *Gazelle Six to Tower, two direct hits. The first vehicle is destroyed. Second vehicle disabled.*

Gazelle Seven — *Tower, that lead truck designated by flares was disabled by an unfriendly rocket.*

Tower — *Gazelles Six and Seven, return to UAE airspace. And good shooting.*

21

———

In Manny's mind, the world might be ending.

The rocket catapulted him thirty feet into air. He flew without spinning, cart-wheeling his arms to keep the earth below his feet, his pants on fire, the zygomatic bone in his cheek cracked from flatbed impact.

The Mercedes plowed through the sand on its nose, threatening to tip over. Its momentum halted and the Mercedes fell down on its charred bottom, and the world continued its mad descent into hell—death from above. The F-16's powerful ammunition couldn't be heard individually, more like a strident scream from the sky. The lead Humvee disintegrated and detonated, and the second used it for a ramp. Manny dropped like a paratrooper into the upslope of a drift as the fighter jet roared a hundred feet overhead.

The fall shocked his feet and tail bone and drove the breath from his lungs, and he was tumbling down the dune in a shower of sand. Exhausted, singed, his eardrums aching, his face beginning hot throbs.

Junior off to his right, trying to run on a broken ankle.

The first Humvee was a smoldering junkyard of flesh

and auto. The second smoked upside down, flattened, one wheel spinning at the air.

Manny sprinted at the flatbed, shouting, his voice unrecognizable. The cabin's nose was crunched in. The windshield and windows were shards in the passengers' laps.

The side door groaned and William Sloan spilled out. Manny caught him; his face bled and his strength was spent and he collapsed into the truck's shade and didn't move.

"Beck! Bronwen!"

"We're alive, love." Bronwen slid her legs toward him and climbed down. Her blouse was shredded by the glass and blood trickled down her neck.

Noelle said something he didn't hear. She wasn't moving. Manny pulled her across the front bench, shoveling sand. A welt already swelled her eye shut where she'd hit the steering wheel. Wedges of glass pierced her shoulder and cheeks, and her forearms twinkled with slivers. Her other eye squeezed against the light, fading now.

He lifted her in his arms and lowered her to the ground next to William. The sun set in the west, giving them enough shade.

She smiled groggily and said her head hurt, but she would live.

"She took quite the knock, brave girl." Bronwen placed her hands on Manny's shoulders as he squatted over Noelle.

Alive. They were all alive.

"Are we out of water?" he said.

William nodded. "I'm afraid so."

Manny cursed. Noelle needed some.

They were out of weapons too, all swallowed by the Empty Quarter.

Junior reached them, sweating, limping.

"I think," murmured Noelle, "we reached the border.

Probably, help is just..." She winced at a pain in her head. "Just over the horizon."

The five of them were too shell-shocked to feel relief. Their escape too narrow. Time existed as a series of terrible events without partitions, which meant another one was coming but they didn't see it, their nerves overworked and numb. They huddled in the shade and panted and thought about water, and ignored their need to hike out. Ignored the pains they felt, the burns and bumps, and ignored the ruined vehicle with bodies unrecognizable fifty yards south, and ignored the upside down Humvee closer, still smoldering, out of which a single figure clawed free like a cockroach.

Junior spotted the piercing headlights of Abu Dhabi's rescue jeeps on the northern horizon. Still two miles away but inbound, and they breathed a collective sigh of relief, and during their vulnerability Liya Al Ariani rose like a wraith on top of the flatbed.

Liya the Signals analyst; Houthi sympathizer; betrayer of her country; survivor of the wreck in the sand; she'd woken with a dislocated shoulder and pulverized ribs, but with her hatred white hot.

Over her clothes she wore an unzipped vest, sewn with explosives and surrounded by fragmentation plates. Liya was a human grenade, and Manny was crouched on the sand too far to stop her.

She screamed, delirious. She would kill herself and the Americans in one fatal blow.

Looking back on it later, Manny could only remember the moment in awful lurches.

"*Almawt li'amrika!*"

Cold fear in Manny's chest.

Bronwen's hands on his shoulders. "Live forever, my love."

Liya's hair matted with blood not her own.

Junior shouting. Noelle squeezing his hand, Noelle beneath him, helpless, blood thundering in Manny's ears.

Liya stepping toward them, her hand holding a control that ran to the vest, moving in slow motion, hateful and hideous.

Bronwen on the flatbed, somehow, a collision with Liya. Wrapping her arms around the zealot.

Jeeps on the horizon, Falcons in the purple over the molten sun, Bronwen and Liya falling backward, live forever, my love, Bronwen bleeding, Bronwen beautiful, both women gone to the far side of the flatbed, carried by Bronwen's strength, Bronwen's life.

Noelle squeezing harder, Junior running around the bumper and falling, running for Bronwen, but the suicide vest activated.

And cratered a shallow hole in the desert. The truck shook and the desert groaned under their feet.

The detonation was so small that the pilots of the F-16s didn't see it. Intended only to destroy nearby *infidels*, the cowardly device did enough, Junior too late, too late by years, Manny crouched over Noelle unmoving, eyes squeezed, Bronwen already gone but her voice warm in his ears.

I'd do it all again, love. This ride of ours

22

The Royal Borough of Windsor and Maidenhead is a short drive from the Heathrow Airport, out of London into the Berkshire countryside. Nobility and yew trees and estates and cottages and English history itself. The dignified homes are ancient but priceless, available only through inheritance.

An entire universe apart from the dry desert in the Middle East.

Not far from Windsor Castle, with a view of livery stables and the River Thames, a chauffeured black car parked in front of a white home two-hundred years old. Two men rose out of the car, one of them wearing a walking boot, and they knocked on the grand home of the Worsley family. The grand home of Bronwen/Alice.

It was nine in the golden morning, and cool.

Mrs. Alexandra Worsley greeted them. Junior she knew. The other man, handsome under the swollen bruises, she recognized. He tried to speak but he couldn't and the emotion he felt came through his eyes, and British rigidity be damned she hugged the man.

Mr. and Mrs. Worsley were presented with a bag of their daughter's things, taken from the Capital Gate hotel. A hair brush, a makeup pouch, blouses, a necklace. Another of the Worsley daughters, so blonde and like her sister that Manny couldn't look at her, sniffed and laughed and said the necklace had been pilfered from her jewelry box, and they cried again.

Junior was under no governmental restraints and he told them Alice Worsley died well, protecting the realm, saving their life from extremists in the Middle East. The two men had buried her there, digging a sandy grave with auto parts as shovels.

A formal funeral would be held at the Bray Parish Cemetery next week.

Mrs. Worsley took Manny's hand and led him to Alice's bedroom. Bronwen's bedroom. Still kept as though she was eighteen. Paintings of angels on the walls. History and warfare books under the nightstand. A small closet stuffed but well organized. On the mirror were taped two photos.

One of Alice with Junior, arms around the other.

One of Alice with Manny, kissing his cheek a year ago inside an airport.

Below the mirror was a larger framed photograph, taken candidly, of Manny alone, laughing.

"This photo. I knew she fancied you then. You were only the second boy to ever get a frame." She wiped her eyes and smiled. "The first, of course, was Prince Harry. She always did prefer the troublemakers, my Alice."

Manny remained there an hour, sitting on the floor.

Would he have married this woman?

Could he have married this woman?

If he ever did marry, it would be for life, come hell or high water. Looking at Alice's life, so different from his, her idyllic canopy bed compared to the cells and hovels he grew up in, he wondered how long the noble girl could've endured him. How long her family could've have endured him.

He knew he was better to look at than live with. Perhaps a man destined to be a dream. Could any woman put up with him for decades?

Morbid thoughts. He felt irritated for turning inward while sitting on the carpet of a martyr.

Speaking of. His eyes latched onto a book about Joan of Arc in the stack under the nightstand. *The Maid and the Queen.* A preference for troublemakers indeed. Had Joan known she was going to die for the cause? It seemed to him like Bronwen had an inkling. That she'd known and followed him anyway. That she thought him worth it.

Was he, though? Was any of this?

Was the hurt worth the work?

Manny's confidence in himself and the order of the universe were shaken. Because he had no answers to questions this empty room demanded of him.

23

———

Later that evening, back in the United States, the care of William Sloan was handed off from Abu Dhabi's finest physicians to Walter Reed National Military Medical Center. His wife and sons were en route, all expenses paid for by the largesse of the Emirates. The man was a hero.

In Roanoke, a black Camaro parked on Windsor Avenue in time for a late homecoming feast, prepared by Mackenzie August on the charcoal grill. Hamburgers and fries and salad and beer. A friendly but subdued dinner, and Junior was a welcomed addition.

The three heroes were exhausted and they turned in early. Tomorrow would be a busy day of debriefing, officials unofficially flying in from Washington to meet them at the marshal's office.

Manny didn't let Noelle leave for her empty apartment. He forced her to take his bed, and he made the couch comfortable for Junior, and he himself laid on an air mattress in Mackenzie's bedroom, the place he slept the deepest.

They tossed and turned, individuals searching for rest but finding only ache and loneliness.

Junior took his bedding to the room where Noelle waited, and he laid on the floor near her door. They listened to each other breathe for an hour until Manny came in too. He slid under the covers with Noelle and she held him, together closer to complete, and the three finally slipped into dreams without remorse.

THE END

Dear Excellent Friend,

Thank you for reading.

That was a tough one.

The Sinatra series is pulp fiction—a sensationalized and action-based thriller. It's intended to be a fun, breezy break from reality. I read a lot of these, growing up, and I hope you enjoy my contribution to the genre.

Clearly the story is not over. There's an upcoming wedding, after all. Rocky and Noelle.

Yes, about that wedding...

It's going to be complicated.

That story might take place in the Mackenzie August mystery series. Have you read it? If not, it's time. At the end of this book there is a fun scene from Book One of the Mackenzie novels, concerning Manny, back when he was a little more broken than he is now.

I had the pleasure of traveling to Abu Dhabi last year, invited by the very William you read about in this novel. An impressive and magnanimous man, as is the UAE in general. I was impressed with their corner of the world, and hope to visit again. If you ever get the chance to travel there, jump on it.

Many thanks to Michael and Carter, experts in all things gallant and MENA. If only the world was full of such men.

<u>What does it take to be a writer?</u>

I get asked this question a lot, so here's my anecdotal advice:

IN HIGH SCHOOL, I read a lot, starting in the 10th grade after discovering *Lord of the Rings* in detention. Quickly I began writing my own narratives, skipping homework to do so. I liked literature so much I majored in English in college, and learned absolutely nothing. Why on earth do we send nineteen-year-olds to college?

I wrote my first full novel when I was 28. It was bad. But that's part of it. You read and read and read, and then you write something bad. That work has since been re-written three times and is now *The Last Teacher*, book zero of the Mackenzie mysteries.

After that, I didn't write again for five years. But I was teaching *Lord of the Flies* three days a week, twice a year for eight years. If my math is correct, I taught that novel forty-eight times. Which means I also taught *Romeo & Juliet* forty-eight times. Without exaggeration, I was still learning from these writers on the forty-eighth iteration, still noticing their craft. For me, that's what it took—teaching masterpieces so thoroughly that I not only understood the story, but could see through the words to the work that went on behind them. Eight years of study and work, which yielded a thousand times more results than a flimsy Bachelors in English.

During the final three years of teaching, I was writing. I wrote young adult literature that was bad, but getting better. After completion of my third novel, my wife and I decided I should retire from teaching and write full-time.

I kept improving. I honed by studying other books and screenplays, something I still do. I think my recent work

Wild South is the best thing I've written, and it was my twenty-sixth novel.

So how does one become a writer—

First, get good at writing, and that could take you a while. You should read the screenplay for *William Clayton* and *Get Out*. You should reread a Hemingway book four times, and *Silence of the Lambs* six times. You absolutely must read (or even better listen to) Robert McKee's book *Story*. And listen to the Story Grid podcast, starting at the beginning. As I write this, I've sold north of half a million books and I'm still learning, still studying, still rereading McKee.

Second, learn to sit for hours at a computer. Yes, hours. Learn to love it. Then go be alive and live an adventure for the rest of the day.

Third, give your best work to people you trust. If they can't get through it, you're not good enough. If they can (doubtful—my friends couldn't), take their advice to heart and keep working and improving. Create something you're proud of, that your friends and family would recommend.

After you've done that, check out Joanna Penn or Mark Dawson or any number of gurus that will guide you through the publishing world. You have options on how to publish.

Most importantly, enjoy the work. Enjoy the reading and studying and sitting and editing and the pure creation. I still do. I *run* to work every day, and can't wait to share the next one with you.

-ALAN

Excerpt from *August Origins*, book one of the Mackenzie mystery series, written seven years ago. Manny has been living with Mackenzie for a week or two—

MY SON HAD a nightmare at two in the morning. Or if not a nightmare, whatever it is that wakes toddlers up with a start in the middle of the night.

Manny leaped to his feet, heavy revolver in his fist.

He was clammy with sweat and the pistol trembled and gleamed. He stared at me and I watched awareness reboot like a computer behind his eyes. Until then, I made no sudden movements. Better safe than shot.

"Sorry," he said.

He dropped the weapon onto his pillow and left the room. I followed. Kix stood in his crib, eyes wet with tears. Manny lifted him and sat in the rocking chair.

"I got him, Mack. Back to bed with you."

Kix seemed puzzled but pacified by this arrangement.

Instead, I laid down on the rug in Kix's room and rubbed at my eye sockets with the heels of my hands. The room was small and smelled like diapers and baby powder. Streetlights threw in rays between the blinds, and the air swirled with dust. The house had that sacred quiet only achieved at two in the morning.

"You having a nightmare too, Manny?"

"Nah. Just, like, this tension I can't let go. Constant stress."

"Do dead bodies ever talk to you? At night?" I asked, thinking about Richard and the North victims.

"At night. And during the day."

"What do they say?"

"Say? Nada. They scream." He chuckled, like a soft snort through his nose. Kix was already fading back to sleep.

I grabbed a stuffed monkey and used it as a pillow. "Why does this happen? I hear dead people too."

"I dunno, amigo. Guilt? Trauma? That's above my pay grade."

"Mine too," I yawned.

"You got faith, right? You should know. Look it up in the Bible."

"I don't think it works that way."

"If you don't know, I got no chance," Manny said.

"I'll ask God. See what he says. But it'll probably be a secret."

"Secret? From me? What, God's a racist?"

"No, he just doesn't like you. Told me so himself," I said.

"He does too. I hope so. I really need the next life to be better than this one."

From my vantage I could see under Kix's crib—pacifiers and stuffed animals. I said, "This one is growing on me."

"We got damaged souls, big Mack. We won't get in to the party upstairs."

"Damaged yet beautiful," I said. "We got a chance. We'll rely on grace."

"That's why we hear the corpses, you know, amigito. Broken souls are the natural consequences of shooting people in the ass. We're paying the price."

"We talk about some deep stuff in the middle of the night, Manuel."

"Wanna smoke?" He yawned so big his jaw cracked. "I could find weed."

"I'm two years clean. I'm good. Kix's asleep, so you go ahead." I stood up and took my son and placed him back in the crib.

"I'm clean for months."

"I'm going back to bed," I said.

"Me too."

"The guest bed might be more comfortable, you know."

"Nah," he said. We shuffled back into my room. "There is no sleep without you."

"You're broken. You should have shot fewer people in the ass."

"I haven't even started yet."

READ AUGUST ORIGINS TODAY! Trust me. If you're only getting started, the Alan Lee Universe is calling.